FAKE LIAR CHEAT

For orders other than by individual consumers, Pocket Books grants a discount on the purchase of **10 or more** copies of single titles for special markets or premium use. For further details, please write to the Vice President of Special Markets, Pocket Books, 1230 Avenue of the Americas, 9th Floor, New York, NY 10020-1586.

For information on how individual consumers can place orders, please write to Mail Order Department, Simon & Schuster Inc., 100 Front Street, Riverside, NJ 08075.

TOD GOLDBERG

FAKE LIAR CHEAT

POCKET
BOOKS

NEW YORK LONDON TORONTO SYDNEY SINGAPORE

An *Original* Publication of MTV Books/Pocket Books

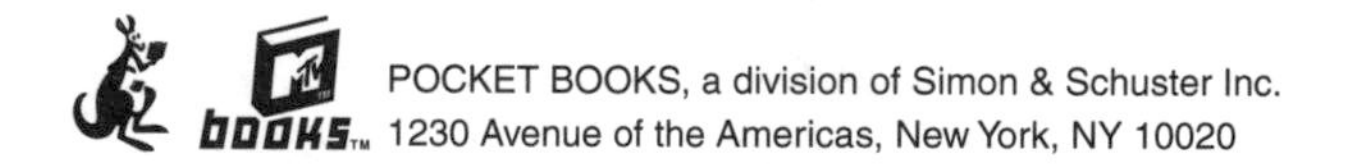
POCKET BOOKS, a division of Simon & Schuster Inc.
1230 Avenue of the Americas, New York, NY 10020

ISBN: 0-7434-0056-9

First MTV Books/Pocket Books trade paperback printing July 2000

10 9 8 7 6 5 4 3 2 1

POCKET and colophon are registered trademarks of Simon & Schuster Inc.

Art direction and design by Deklah Polansky
Photography by Jason Stang

Printed in the U.S.A.

For Wendy, who sacrificed so that I could dream.

Acknowledgments

I am so grateful to be able to acknowledge the many people who helped make this book possible:

Tom Filer, who is a brilliant teacher and a better friend. Without Tom, my words would not have found a page. This book is as much his as it is mine. Equal thanks are due to Tom's Goat Alley Workshop for reading everything I've written and for forcing me to strive for something better.

My family has supported and loved me all along the way—even when it was certainly difficult—and never stopped believing in me. Although to most of them I'm just a little kid with peanut butter on his face. . . .

Humble thanks go to my friends who have always felt like family—Todd, Jim, Dave and Vitaly—for keeping me in the right spirits, and many of the wrong ones.

I am indebted to my wonderful agent, Jennie Dunham, for knowing all the rational things to say when my moods shifted wildly, my blood sugar dropped, I filled with self-doubt, and it appeared that the world was going to end. She is a rare combination of warmth and honesty and I'm lucky to have her representing me.

Gracious thanks are due to my editor, Paul Schnee, for believing in this novel and taking a chance on me. He always makes me feel like a writer, which is pretty cool.

Finally, I owe every word to Wendy. For telling me it would happen just as we'd planned, and that if it didn't, it wouldn't really matter.

FAKE LIAR CHEAT

Prologue

We sit in restaurants creating, modifying, extracting. There are deals to be made, lies to be told, directions to be taken. There are so many things we need to consider, she says. She says this a lot.

She says it in a bistro in Santa Monica.

She says it speeding on the 101 freeway.

We lie to each other in fourteen restaurants in six different cities. We lie in front of embarrassed waiters and alone in lobbies. "Your opinion," Claire says, "is not based on research. Mine is."

Sometimes, I order for her. "Give the lady the lobster bisque, but make sure the lobster is fresh."

She leans across the aisle and touches a gentleman on the elbow. "Excuse me," she says. "I just wanted to say how fantastic you were in Spielberg's last movie. Very moving."

I move among them. I listen for the way they enunciate words. There is a woman I see at the Mondrian who always pronounces Los Angeles, "Lost Angels." She seems to get a big kick out of it. I don't copy her.

There are places that I go to when we are not together. I am still very much me there. Still young and alive and unambitious.

There is love here, I think.

I name our unborn children and debate their futures.

"Maybe when this is all over," Claire says, "I'll become a relationship counselor."

"That would be foolish," I say. She knows this. I know this. It is part of the game.

What we are going through is nothing if not normal. Relationships marred by strife work, says one of my friends, because even boxers hug after fighting. Opposition, he adds, creates passion.

"We are like dark and light then," I say.

"No," Claire says. "Dark is not the opposite of light; it is the absence of light."

It sounds contrived, but that is how she speaks.

So I continue to add the costs, make the decisions, and prepare.

We've been playing this game for more than a month. It works very simply. She calls all the shots.

"Tell me about this movie deal you've been working on," she says.

Wisps of hair dangle around her ears and play toward her cheeks.

I want to touch her. I want to slip my lips over hers and cradle her words in my mouth. She knows this. She knows everything.

"It's not much," I say. "We're looking to top out at a hundred mil." I feel their eyes on me. They are subtle because they hear this kind of talk nightly. But not from me. They've never seen me on *Entertainment Tonight.*

So we plan. We devise. We lie. We fake. And she cheats. She cheats everyone she meets. Everyone has a secret. Hers, Claire's, is out in the open—a gradual climax of details that brings me here, now, tonight. A debt paid in full, but at what price?

How much does it cost to feel beloved? And do we even get what we want from this world? And how does it all prepare me for tonight? For right now when I have this woman sitting beside me, sirens flashing in my rearview mirror and the police have placed spikes in the road to stop my car.

There are so many things we need to consider.

One

I work on the sixth floor of a high-rise building in Century City. The company I work for—Staff Genius—is fairly successful and they consider me an up-and-coming young star.

My job is to interview and place applicants in temporary jobs that best suit their skills. Staff Genius pays me two thousand dollars a month just to show up each morning, and then I earn commission based on a percentage of the temp's pay. Basically, my wages are dependent on people who have either been fired from their last jobs or can't find jobs.

"Lonnie," my manager says to me. "Can I see you in my office?"

I get up from my desk, where I've only been pretending to work, straighten my tie, and go over a mental checklist of excuses. *She seemed right for the job. His typing was very fast. I think the client misunderstood the qualifications the candidate needed.* When in doubt, blame the client.

"Take a seat," my manager says. Her name is Julie. She has been working in the temp business, she likes to tell us, since before there were typewriters. It's an exaggeration, but Julie does look old. She wears skirts that are too tight for her sagging body and smokes cigarettes in her office. We are a nonsmoking facility. "Lonnie, I want to talk to you about career opportunities within Staff Genius."

I erase my mental checklist of excuses and pull down my checklist of blatant lies that will possibly improve my financial standing. "That would be great, Julie," I say.

"First of all," she says and then lights a cigarette. The venetian blinds in her office are yellow from all the smoke. "You've really buckled down as far as getting here on time and then staying late goes. I appreciate it and I know the clients appreciate it."

I look at her seriously. But I'm thinking: C'mon, Julie. Let's hear the money talk.

"And the way you handle the temps has steadily improved," Julie says. The first rule Staff Genius has, and this is unwritten, is that the temps are not your friends. They are not your equals. They are a means to a very discernible end. Don't flirt. Don't fraternize. Don't trust. "They fear you now, Lonnie. You make them show up on time."

"I like to keep the trains running," I say. Julie smiles. She isn't exactly a student of history.

"And let me tell you," Julie says, "Corporate has seen your numbers jump." Corporate operates out of Jacksonville. The only thing they see is numbers. On occasion, Corporate sends their people to visit our branch. They give us pep talks, pass out logo buttons, pump us full of Staff Genius propaganda—*We are seriously evaluating the idea of casual Fridays*—and then leave. "They were very impressed by the way you held the office together when I was out with the shingles."

For the two weeks Julie was bedridden with the virus, I was in charge of the outside sales staff and Charlie, the other placement coordinator. We came in every morning at ten and left every evening before four. We played loud rap music during the day. Charlie got so drunk at lunch one afternoon that he threw up on the Xerox machine and made copies of it. I told the outside sales staff they didn't have to come in. They chose not to.

"I enjoyed the responsibility," I say.

"So," Julie says, "I've recommended you for a management position at the new satellite office in Encino."

"That would be tremendous," I say. There is nothing I would rather not do.

"It will be a lot of work and I won't be there to hold your hand."

"I realize that," I say.

"Now this won't happen for another two months," Julie says. "So just keep on pumping up your numbers."

"You know I will."

Julie stands up, shakes my hand, and then opens the door for me. I quell my desire to run screaming from her office and instead excuse myself to the rest room.

Charlie is reading a magazine in one of the stalls. I see his feet and hear pages turning.

I knock on the stall door.

"Lonnie, that you?"

"Yeah."

The toilet flushes. "So," Charlie says, stepping out. "You fired or promoted?"

"Worse."

"Oh," Charlie says. "Transferred?"

"Kind of. They want me to manage Encino."

Charlie goes to the sink and washes his hands. He dries them on his pants. An issue of *Popular Mechanics* is folded and stuffed into his back pocket. "A position of power," he says. "Don't go Genghis Khan on me."

"I don't even want the job," I say. "But the money will help pay the bills."

"Selling crack pays the bills. This makes you downright respectable."

Charlie and I celebrate my new misfortune by drinking shots of tequila after work. I drive home on the 405 with a buzz so thick that everything takes on a soft, fuzzy focus. I remember an old drunk-driving trick from college and put my car on cruise control five miles below the speed limit. Now I only have to concentrate on keeping a straight line. A Highway Patrol officer passes me without even looking in my direction.

When I come over the top of Mulholland and see the twinkling spread of the San Fernando Valley below me, I can't help but think that someday this will all be mine. Layers of yellow smog, seven shopping malls, one million people, and countless unemployed workers looking for temporary jobs.

All mine.

I pull off on the Ventura Boulevard exit and vomit in the parking lot of an El Pollo Loco.

We meet at a Barnes and Noble after I accidentally spill my mocha frappuccino on the cover of her Yale Shakespeare.

"Jesus," she says. "What kind of moron are you?"

"The kind who will buy you another book," I say. She doesn't say anything. I stare at her for what seems to me like a very long time. I know there are bones beneath her skin, but right now she looks like a ghost. When she does smile, I feel something twinge in my stomach.

She stands up to see if any frappuccino has gotten on her expensive business suit. It hasn't. "Well," she says and then makes an exaggerated look over both of her shoulders. No one is watching us. She leans forward and whispers, "You don't need to buy the book. I haven't bought it yet."

She slips her arm through mine and begins chatting me up as though we are husband and wife. "Did you pick up the kids? I think the dog has worms. I invited the Andersons over for dinner." Before I really understand what is happening, we are standing outside and she is holding the Yale Shakespeare volume, all 800 pages and $65 worth, under one arm.

"That's a pretty slick maneuver," I say. "Do you usually work alone?"

"I don't make a habit of shoplifting, if that's what you're asking." We are standing next to a convertible black Saab, and she tosses the book into the backseat. "I can certainly afford to buy a book." That much is certainly true. Her car is maybe a '91, but at one time she had to pay $35,000 for it. I take inventory: diamond earrings, Cartier watch, triple-banded gold necklace; her suit alone cost more than I put down on my car. My final cursory check of her jewelry finds no wedding ring.

"I'd love to work with you again," I say, extending my hand. "I'm Lonnie."

"Claire." Her palm is warm and soft against mine and I don't want to let go of it. I hold on.

"Do you think I could call you sometime?" I ask, holding her for just a moment longer than I should.

"No," Claire says, "you don't have my number." She gets into her car and starts the engine. I stand there and just stare at her because I can't think what else I should do. "Do you have a business card or something, Lonnie?" I fumble through my wallet and find one of my Staff Genius cards and hand it to her. She reads it for a moment. "'Account Manager,'" she says. "Color me impressed. I'll be in touch."

Claire calls on a Tuesday afternoon when Charlie and Julie are out to lunch.

"I didn't think you'd call," I say. "I thought I kind of freaked you or something."

"Because you held my hand too long or because you stared at me like I was a meal?" It feels like every wall in my office has jumped forward and the air has become thick and hot. I loosen my tie. "Either way," she says, "it was flattering."

I don't say anything—again—because everything is too close.

"Do you have plans tonight?" Claire asks.

"No."

"No big Staff Genius mixer?"

"There are only a few of us," I say, "and we're already familiar with each other." She laughs then, but not at me. I don't think.

"Meet me at Intermezzo around nine for dinner," she says. "Do you know where that is?"

"Yes," I lie.

"Don't valet," she says and hangs up.

I relay my story to Charlie when he gets back from lunch. He smells as if he might have had a beer with his tuna sandwich.

"Intermezzo is pretty pricey," he says. "I used to take first dates there. Lotta Hollywood types and bottled water."

"How much can I look to spend?"

Charlie looks at me like I'm a madman. "This is the nineties, bro. She made the initial call, she made the initial date, she initials the credit card receipt. Simple formula."

"I can't do it that way," I say.

"Suit yourself," Charlie says. "But it's bad precedent for the rest of us."

I have two pairs of black pants that I consider fashionable, three pairs of khaki pants that make me look like an ad for J. Crew, and several dress shirts suitable for the office but unsuitable for the Hollywood in-crowd. I try on everything I own. I mix and match. I button my dress shirts up to my collar and strike model poses.

I call my sister, Karen.

"Just don't wear a turtleneck," she says. "You'll look like a fag."

It's seven forty-five. I put on the least wrinkled, most fashionable of my two pairs of black pants and an undershirt. I drive to Charlie's apartment and pound on the door.

"Sweet Christ," Charlie says. "How about a little less cologne. You smell like a hooker."

"I need to borrow a shirt," I say. "Something cool."

"Pick whatever," Charlie says, leading me to his bedroom and opening his closet door. "Just promise to wash it when you're through."

It's eight-fifteen and I am going blind staring into a closet filled with ugly shirts.

"I need help," I say. "I've gotta be over the hill in forty-five."

Charlie pulls a purple silk shirt off a hanger and hands it to me. "This shirt is a magnet. I've worn it to Intermezzo a handful of times. Just take your undershirt off and you're straight."

When I put the shirt on, it feels soft on my chest. It feels like Claire's handshake. "I like it," I say.

"Three words for you if you get busy in it," Charlie says. "Dry. Clean. Only."

It takes me ten minutes to find a parking place on Melrose. When I walk into the restaurant Claire is sitting at a table drinking wine.

"Sorry I'm late," I say.

"You didn't valet, did you?"

"No." Claire smiles. This is something she does often, I think. Her teeth are perfect symmetry. She reaches across the table and touches my hand.

"Why are you shaking?"

"I didn't know I was," I say. She is still touching my hand when the waiter comes by and asks if I'd like something to drink. "Just water," I start to say, but Claire cuts me off.

"Bring us a bottle of merlot," she says, then takes the wrist of the waiter into her free hand. "And make it your best." She holds him for a moment, and I'm just an accessory. The waiter looks at Claire's hand on his wrist. I see color rise in his cheeks. She is touching him because he is there. "Thank you," Claire says, and the waiter is gone.

"You look very nice, Claire," I say.

"Don't say my name!"

"What?"

"Don't call me Claire," she whispers.

I'm confused, anxious. I feel as if all the conversations in the restaurant have been turned up a thousand decibels.

"She couldn't have said *that,"* a woman says.

"Word for word," another woman says.

I want to put my hands over my ears to drown out the sound, to stop the conversations from running over me, but I see Claire is leaning forward. She touches my hand again.

"You didn't think I was going to *pay* for this," Claire says, throwing herself against the air with laughter. "Did you?"

"No," I say. I understand now. This is not a date. She is touching me because she touches everyone. She stretches herself out and touches the waiter. She touches her silverware. Her glass. She is part of a scene. I am a bit player.

"Now," Claire says quietly. "Choose a name. We need to make this real."

"Right," I say.

"And no true stories, nothing anyone can overhear that will matter."

"Of course," I say, remembering our conversation inside Barnes and Noble. We are working together again.

"The flight in was horrible," Claire says loudly. "Five hours of screaming children and an overbooked first class. I wasn't about to take coach."

"I know what that's like." I pause for a moment, seeing that the couple next to us is listening. "That's why I bought the Gulf Stream," I say. "Hell, I'd rather drop a couple hundred grand into a plane than deal with that kind of noise."

This is not my skin.

These are not my words.

I feel electric.

Claire lifts the wine glass to her lips and drinks. I pour her more expensive wine.

I order grilled salmon, covered in shallots on a bed of garlic spinach. Price: $63. Claire orders the broiled lamb salad, served warm, and escargot. Price: $80.

"An excellent choice," our waiter says. He is model handsome. Claire lets her eyes linger over his body.

Former teen idol Rick Springfield is having a glass of iced tea and a small dinner salad. Robert Urich is waiting at the bar for a table. Jennifer Love Hewitt is drinking Evian water.

Claire motions for a busboy. "More wine," she says to him. We've already finished two bottles, at a hundred bucks a pop.

"You need to go shopping," Claire says. "That shirt should be thrown out."

"There isn't a Gucci shop in Houston," I say. "And I like to be comfortable when I'm piloting the jet. So I just dug this out of the closet."

Claire lets a smile dart around the edges of her mouth.

We drink another two hundred dollars' worth of wine and then order dessert. Claire gets the chef's specialty, tiramisu. I order the crème brûlée. After dessert, but before we order our complimentary coffee, Claire goes to the bathroom to call a cab. The restaurant is packed. There are a hundred people eating dinner, another forty in the bar, and maybe another twenty-five waiting outside because they don't know anyone.

Our waiter drops off the check. He looks disappointed that Claire is away from the table.

"Great service," I say.

"It was my pleasure."

I pick up the check. $727.95.

The balance of my checking account is $521.13. I haven't paid my Visa bill in two months.

Twenty minutes later, the bill stuffed into Claire's purse, we walk out of the restaurant. Claire sticks her head into the kitchen and thanks the chef on the way out. "Brilliant again," she says.

We slide through the tight mob out front and find our cab parked in the red zone. The cabdriver takes us to our cars. I pay him twenty dollars.

"I'll call you," Claire says and is gone.

■ ■ ■

For three days, I wait by the phone. I'm not paranoid, but I like to think people say what they mean.

On day four, Claire calls me at eight in the morning.

"I hope I didn't wake you," she says.

"Not at all," I say. "I was just sitting here waiting for the phone to ring."

"I've been really busy," she says.

"Me too," I lie.

"Cremation is nothing compared to the week I've had," Claire says. I don't respond. It's like she is talking to someone else.

"Do you want to see me again?" Claire asks. Her voice is low now, something near a purr, and it makes me press the phone closer to my ear.

"I do," I say, before I even know I have said it.

"Not a couples thing," she says. "Just you and me."

Three

We dress in our finest clothes and eat at the finest restaurants. We meet for lunch on the weekends and dine next to movie stars and the people who make the movies. We drive our own cars but park them blocks away. We reserve cabs that arrive at just the right time to pick us up. We pay for nothing.

"I'll have what Arnold is having," I say.

"I don't want anything that is being served to anyone else," she says. "Tell the chef to make me something special."

I kiss women I've never met on both cheeks and tell them they look wonderful. Claire presses herself against producers and whispers things into their ears that make them blush. I watch her constantly. There is an assurance in the way she brushes her hair from her face and applies her lipstick. Every movement has a reason.

She is like a monument preserved for me. A national treasure.

There are times when she will grab my hand and hold it against her leg as we walk. We are never each other in these times. I can never say to her that I sent a convicted burglar out on a temp job. I can never confess to her that sometimes I dial from memory the numbers of all my ex-girlfriends and hang up before anyone can answer.

But I choose this. I choose to run out of restaurants without paying. I choose to watch her drive away in her Saab while I sit in my five-speed manual transmission Tercel.

We are friends, but I know no more about her than the first day we met. I know that when she walks, people want to open a path for her. When she talks to me, even in this fantasy world we have, I am in love. I am in love with the way her voice slips into a drawl when she isn't concentrating. I am in love with the beautiful lines around her face and the dissonance in her smile.

We are friends—not because I choose it, though. With Claire, nothing is up to me at all.

"The partner wanted me out," the applicant says. Her hair is cropped close to her scalp and she is wearing hoop earrings that could accommodate flames and leaping dogs. I squint down at her application.

"Was this at Glickman and Brown or at Rosenthal, Narvid, and Jones?"

"Both," she says. Her name is Rosie Klinger and she claims to be a legal secretary. "Do you mind?" she says, reaching into a jar of mints on my desk and popping one into her mouth. "You see," she says, "old man Brown and his wife split and he thought I would be his 'rebound.' I'm not like that, you know what I'm saying?"

"Uh-huh."

"And so he starts talking about how I missed this filing date and this discovery deadline and on and on," Rosie says. "So I finally say to him that I'm not his lapdog and so on and so forth and he kicks me to the curb."

"But isn't it your job to keep those dates lined up?" I ask.

Rosie squares in her seat and takes another mint. "Oh, so that's how it is here? I get it."

"I'm just saying," I start to say, but then I smell *her*. Vanilla and lilacs. I look up and Claire is standing in the lobby. Her body, lean and tan, seems to float in the folds of her sundress. I can make out the soft curve of her clavicle. Her hair is pulled back into a ponytail. She waves at me over the receptionist's head and my mouth turns suddenly very dry.

"You all right, Mr. Staff Genius?" Rosie asks. "Because I'm still waiting for you to tell me what you're saying."

Claire takes a pen from the receptionist and writes something on a piece of paper, then folds it over. The receptionist brings it to me. It says: LUNCH?

"What I was saying, Ms. Klinger, is that I don't think I can help you. My associate Charlie, however, might have something for you in the clerical field." Charlie turns around, a Twix bar shoved in his mouth, and I hand him Rosie's file.

As I walk out with Claire, I hear Charlie tell Rosie that we have several positions open in the meat-packing industry.

16

We are driving down Wilshire in her Saab with the top down. It is June and we have known each other for a month. I am desperately in love with her when she wears sundresses, madly in love with her when she wears anything else. We are friends right now, but I have no idea what she does for a living.

When we go out to perpetrate our little scams, I call her Madeline and she calls me Jake. She is an opera singer from the East and I am a former real-estate developer from Texas who now owns his own production company. Never mind that I have never stepped foot in Texas and that I'm only twenty-eight.

Before I meet Claire at the various restaurants, I read *Variety* and the *Hollywood Reporter* so that I know what the entertainment buzz is. I also read the real-estate section of the *Times* so I can advise my friend the opera singer about land bargains I've been tipped to.

It is tough to play this part at first because, as Claire points out, I don't have the wardrobe. I go to Venice Beach and buy, for seven dollars, an imitation diamond Rolex. I go to Marshalls and purchase, on sale, seven butterfly-collared shirts and several pairs of those heavily pleated pants that seem to be the style of choice for Hollywood Iranians and hipsters. From far away, I look the part. Stare close enough and you see that my silk shirts are rayon and my linen pants are plain old cotton.

Today, however, in Claire's convertible Saab, I am wearing my work clothes. My thirty-dollar white button-down from Macy's and my favorite houndstooth slacks aren't exactly *haute couture*. "Where to today?" I ask. "Spago?"

"No," Claire says. "I thought we'd just go to McDonald's and get to know each other." She pats my thigh gingerly. It feels as if I've been stuck with a cattle prod. For a month we have played out this charade and I have gone along because at some point I thought a stolen dinner at Toscana might lead to a night of stolen passion in the backseat of a cab. I thought that one night I would rent a Navy uniform and we would pretend that I was on the Joint Chiefs of Staff and she was my KGB counterpart and we were forced to copulate to save the world.

What I didn't think was that she wanted me for more than a night of stupid fun; that she was interested in me beyond the false adventures I could provide. So, when Claire left her hand on my thigh and pulled into the McDonald's in Westwood, I began to understand that nothing was quite what I had believed it to be.

"So what makes you qualified," Claire says, "to judge people for these jobs that you know nothing about?"

"I went to college," I say. "I know how things work in a logical fashion." We are sitting outside in the McDonald's Playland eating cheeseburgers and fries. Claire paid for both meals since I didn't have any cash on me.

"That woman in your office," she says. "You just decided right there that she was not going to get a job. Don't you consider that she might have a child to support or a mortgage to pay?"

"No," I say. "I've got my own problems. If I decide that I can't depend on her to pay for my child or my mortgage, then she doesn't get a job."

Claire sets down her cheeseburger and opens her eyes extremely wide. "You have a child?"

"I'm speaking hypothetically."

"Oh, well, if you had a child, that would be fine," she says. "Don't get me wrong." A woman dressed far too well for McDonald's walks into the Playland with two screaming boys and an overweight Mexican woman. The Mexican woman and the well-dressed woman have a conversation in Spanish that ends with the Mexican woman sitting down and the well-dressed woman climbing back into a Mercedes-Benz and driving off. Claire follows the well-dressed woman with her eyes the whole way. "That isn't right," she says. "If you have kids, you take care of them. You don't leave them at McDonald's where some strange couple might steal them."

Kidnapping is where I draw the line, I'm thinking, but then Claire giggles. She does have parameters. "Lonnie," she says, leaning across the table so that her face is only inches from my own, "I think I'm pretty happy we know each other." She brushes her lips against mine. "Buy an extra toothbrush tonight."

A large health-care company calls my office at four-thirty and orders several executive secretaries for the next morning. Charlie and I make calls to every available worker we have and turn up very little.

"What about that loon we interviewed this afternoon?" Charlie says. "She's got the skills."

"Rosie Klinger? She'd burn the place down." I stare at my computer screen and scroll past names of people who are out of work. People who, for some reason, find it incredibly difficult to work nine to five without incident.

"So," Charlie says. "That was *the* girl?"

I nod. All I've told Charlie is that she intrigues me.

"If that dress she had on was any thinner," Charlie says, "I would have seen what she ate for breakfast."

"Well," I say, "she has a nice body and likes to show it, I guess. Nothing wrong with that."

"Got any fingerprints on her?" Charlie asks.

"For what?"

"My buddy will run a DMV on her for twenty bucks," Charlie says. "Save you some revenge time in case she dumps your ass."

Julie walks out of her office and sees Charlie and me chatting while one of our largest customers thinks we are searching for the perfect executive secretaries. "Oh, you two have time to bullshit?" We don't say anything. Charlie just gives Julie his "I'm innocent of all crimes, Officer" look. She turns to me. "Lonnie, give me some names."

I look down at the order form in front of me, which is blank, and say the first two names that pop into my head. "Uh, Rosie Klinger and Claire, uh," I don't know her last name. "Claire, uh, just Claire."

"What kind of name is that?" Julie says. "Claire Adjustclaire?"

"No," I say and feel something start to rise in my stomach. "Like Madonna. Just one name. She's an aspiring actress."

Julie leans over my desk and picks up the order and reads it. "Okay, then, I'll call HealthMerge and let them know we have two people so far and that the other names are forthcoming. Right?"

Charlie gives Julie a salute. "Yes, ma'am. O Captain, my Captain!" Julie waves her cigarette at him and closes her office door. "Brilliant move, Lonnie," Charlie says after Julie is safely in her office and on the phone. "Why didn't you just say Napoleon?"

When I get home at nine o'clock, there is a message from Claire on my machine. She says to come over and to bring clothes for work tomorrow. She leaves me directions to her home, which is in an expensive neighborhood in Brentwood. My face feels very warm. I have not told Claire that she, too, is working tomorrow. For that matter, I don't know if she has a job at all. I do know that at some point tomorrow, Rosie Klinger will be sitting next to someone, maybe even Claire, talking about being some lawyer's lapdog and I will be very nervous.

I also know that I am nervous right now; that the last time I had sex with an animate object was six months previous. I also know that Claire has something over me, a control that makes me want to do things for her, to find out why she lives in an expensive neighborhood, drives an expensive car, and goes around town stealing meals with me at expensive restaurants.

I also know, more than anything, that there is a desperation in me that won't allow me to ask about any of this. I am captured by Claire. By her smell. By her clothes. By the way she glides when she walks and makes every room she stands in seem to be in motion.

She makes me feel like I am moving. Like I am someone who can drift into any world that I choose and do whatever I want.

My sister, Karen, calls just as I finish stuffing an overnight bag. "Mom is coming into town on Monday," she says. "She wants to go out to dinner."

"Okay," I say. "Just let me know where and I'll show up."

"I might bring Michael," Karen says. Michael is her boyfriend. "Just in case conversation lags. Why don't you bring Connie."

"It's Claire," I say, "and we're just friends."

"Whatever," Karen says. "I'll talk to you before Monday."

I hang up and check myself in the mirror. My face is sweaty, as if I've been running. I sit down on my cheap IKEA couch and turn on the TV. I need to give myself time to cool off. Dinner on Monday with Mom. I'm sure Claire would love to meet my family.

Channel 9 news is on and they are interviewing a man who lost $50,000 at an Indian casino in Palm Springs. He is smiling. He is laughing. He says it made him feel expensive. He says it made him feel like he was one of those people you see on TV. He says he'd do it again just for the feeling of excitement.

I drive to Claire's so quickly it feels like I am moving the ground.

Four

There is a gate that stretches ten feet high in front of Claire's house. I check the address again and there is no mistaking it: Claire lives two houses away from O.J. Simpson's old home. There are closed-circuit security cameras mounted on the top of a brick wall and when my car pulls close, the gates open.

I park behind Claire's Saab and walk up a long, cobble-lined driveway that leads to the front door. There are cameras everywhere. I feel like a high-class cat burglar or a diamond smuggler. When I look back and see my 1992 Toyota Tercel parked under glossy yellow lamps and on expensive bricks, I understand completely that I get temporary jobs for people.

Claire is standing at the door when I get there.

"Any trouble finding it?"

"No," I say. "It's pretty hard to miss."

"It's comfortable," she says and I walk in.

The house is two stories and several thousand square feet. I follow Claire down a long hallway that is punctuated with marble flooring and expensive paintings. I can hear music coming from somewhere in the house. It sounds like someone is practicing the violin behind closed doors.

"That's beautiful music," I say. "Who plays?"

"It's pumped in," Claire says. "I think it tends to be a bit annoying." She stops walking and we are standing in front of a closed door. She puts her hand on my cheek. "You're sweating," she says.

"I'm a little nervous," I say.

Claire frowns—not a sad frown or a scary frown, but a frown that makes me think that she's been in this place before. "I don't bite, Lonnie."

"It's just that," I start, but then Claire's lips are pressed against mine. And this is a real kiss, not the peck she gave me at McDonald's. She is pressing herself against me and opening the door behind her. I feel racy—like if I make the wrong move my heart will explode. I keep my eyes open because I want to remember all of this. The way she looks up close. The way her bedroom rushes into focus when the door opens. The delicate way Claire touches my face.

She pulls away from me and sits down on her bed. She is all poise again. "See," she says. "Harmless." I am standing in the doorway still, my duffel bag over my shoulder. Her bedroom is ornate. There is a four-poster bed made from oak. She has an antique rolltop desk that houses an expensive computer and printer. There is an open closet filled with clothes—outfits I've seen her in.

"What do you use the computer for?" I ask, after it becomes apparent that I don't know what to say.

"Nothing," she says. "It's just a toy." I set my bag down and sit next to Claire. Our knees touch. I feel very warm. She puts her hand on my thigh. "Lonnie, calm down, okay?"

"I don't really know you," I say. Claire looks hurt. "I mean, I guess we're starting to know each other, and that's fine. This is just odd."

"You know where I live. You know my name."

"Actually, I have no idea what your last name is."

Claire laughs harder than I've ever heard her laugh. "It's Gooden," she says finally. "Claire Gooden."

"Lonnie Milton," I say and we shake hands. This time I let go in an appropriate amount of time. "Pleased to meet you."

"Likewise," Claire says. Then she kisses me again, softly. "I like the way your lips feel. You kiss correctly."

I get up and look out the large picture window behind her desk. I can see my Tercel and Claire's Saab. There are no other cars. "Do you live here alone?"

"Sometimes," Claire says, then she is behind me, hugging me. I feel awkward and large with her small frame against mine. This affection makes me feel jittery. For a month I have done nothing but fantasize about Claire. I've created elaborate scenarios where we would end up in precisely this position. But now, when I can feel her breasts against my back and her breath on my neck, I want to dive through the window just to feel the glass.

She reaches her hand up and places it on my chest. "Your heart is racing," she says. Outside, a police car pulls up to the front gate and shines a bright light over the driveway. It scans back and forth twice and then is gone.

"Why am I here?" I ask. I hear Claire sigh behind me.

"Because I invited you," she says, turning me around. My back is against the window and I think that if I press hard enough it will shatter. Glass will rain down on the brick driveway. The police will return and I will be hauled off to jail for impersonating someone with wealth.

I picture it then, as Claire looks into my eyes, the police handcuffing me on the expansive driveway. They call me a fake, a liar, a cheat. They ask me about a string of unsolved dine-and-ditch cases plaguing Los Angeles.

They call me a fake again and again.

Claire kisses me. Her hand slides down the length of my back and over my legs. I feel electric.

The police haul me in front of a judge and all I can tell him is that I'm afraid this isn't my skin. Someone else is inside me.

We fall onto the bed. My duffel bag is kicked to the floor and the zipper splits open, spilling my toiletries onto the carpet. I smell my cologne leaking out. The bottle of Paco Rabanne my mother bought me my senior year of college is pooling beneath the bed. "It's time you smelled like a man, not a frat boy," Mom said.

Until tonight, I've never worn the cologne. Until tonight when the police place the cuffs around my wrists, the judge indicts me for dinner theft, and Claire Gooden slips her tongue into my ear do I wear Paco Rabanne, Eau de Toilet pour Hommes.

There is a mirror above the sink in Claire's bathroom. I'm brushing my teeth when I see my reflection in it. I look the same. Brown hair, brown eyes, brown stubble. I brush my tongue for a solid minute. It is the same pink it has always been. There are still a million tastebuds. I still gag when the toothbrush reaches too far into my throat. There are still molars with silver fillings on them that Dr. Crane put in the week before he died of heart failure.

But I feel different.

I wash my face with hot water and walk back into the bedroom. Claire is facedown on the bed, her brown hair fanned out over her back. I think she is asleep. It is nearly midnight. I have to be in my office in eight hours.

This is a big deal.

"Claire," I say and I shake her. "Wake up, baby." She turns over and looks up at me with utter fear. She jumps out of bed, dragging the comforter with her.

"Who are you?" she screams. "How'd you get into my bed?" She backs herself into a corner of the room and pulls the comforter under her chin.

"Claire," I say. "It's me. Lonnie. You're asleep."

Claire squeezes her forehead in a tight grip and shakes her head. "Jesus," she says. "I'm sorry." She walks back to the bed and gets in. "That happens sometimes. I'm not used to having you in bed with me, I guess."

"It's okay," I say. She starts to close her eyes again. "Claire, don't go to sleep. I need to ask you for a favor."

"Honey," she says, "we've got the rest of our lives. Let's just sleep now."

"No," I say. "Not like that. I need you to go to a job for me tomorrow."

Claire sits up in bed. She's awake now. "What are you talking about, Lonnie?"

I explain it to her.

"I've never typed a single word," she says. "Much less taken orders from anyone."

"Don't you work?"

Claire gets up and grabs a T-shirt from the closet and puts it on. When she gets back into bed, she is angry. "I can't believe you, Lonnie." I put my hand on her stomach and she brushes it away. "This isn't something I want to talk about right now. If I knew that you needed a résumé from me I would have had something prepared."

"Maybe I should go," I say. Maybe I should dive out that window and run to my car.

"No," she says. "I'll do it. Just don't ask me to do something like this again."

"I wouldn't," I say. "All I need is your social security number."

Claire glares at me, her eyes narrowing into sharp ovals. "What," she says, "are you going to run a credit check on me now?"

"So you can get paid," I say.

"This is deceptive, Lonnie. I don't think I like you being deceptive." Claire leans over and turns off the light. In minutes she is sleeping, her breath coming in short, husky rasps. I stare up at the ceiling in the dark, counting.

One. Two. Three.

Breath.

One. Two. Three.

Breath.

I remember the first time I spent the night with a girl. I remember watching her fall asleep and then touching her hair and her lips and her nose. Just tracing each of her features into my fingers. Making a connection. In the morning the girl asked me if I had slept well and I told her that I had never spent a better night in bed.

I trace Claire's breath into my mind.

I like her deception. I know she likes mine.

We are no longer friends.

Five

Charlie is sitting at his desk eating a muffin and reading the paper when I walk in. His tie is off and he has his feet on the desk. His computer isn't on. It is 9:05.

"What's going on?" I ask.

"Julie called in sick," Charlie says. "Some kinda bronchial infection. She wants you to call her."

"Great," I say and dial Julie's number.

"Lonnie," Julie says after she picks up her phone and hacks out a few thick coughs. "You're late."

"Sorry, I can't always predict traffic."

"Whatever," she says. "Listen to me. I've got some kind of lung problem today."

"Probably from smoking," I say because I feel as if I can just float into this world of Julie's and make it mine.

"No," she says, ignoring me, "it's my damn swamp cooler. Be a doll, Lonnie, and make sure everything runs smoothly over at HealthMerge today."

"I feel we sent over some excellent candidates," I say.

"Go over there at lunch and make sure," Julie says. "I talked to Corporate last night, and they are very excited about all this business HealthMerge is giving us. It would look good for your file."

"Sure thing," I say and we hang up.

"So," Charlie says, "martinis for lunch?"

"No," I say and then tell him my lunch plans.

"Ever the Corporate zealot," Charlie says, then picks up his paper and heads to the rest room.

I sit at my desk and stare at my telephone. I think that at some point today it will ring and my job will be on the line.

Claire woke me with a kiss on the lips. She was leaning over me, her hair touching my face. There's a bagel on the desk for you, she said. I took out some cream cheese and some butter, she said, because I don't know what you prefer. I wrote my social on a Post-it, she said, it's right there on the nightstand.

She walked across the room and I saw that she was wearing a light-colored business suit and conservative pumps. It's seven-thirty, she said, I don't know what time you need to leave here.

I was still asleep. I was still dreaming that I had made love to Claire. I was still Jake and she was still Madeline and we were still nothing.

Then she kissed me again. And again. And I was awake and my dream was real and she was taking off that light-colored suit and those conservative shoes and we were moving against each other. She was pulling at the hair on my chest and on the back of my neck and all I could think about was that this was right. That infatuation aside, that possible blind love aside, Claire knew how to create movement. Claire could touch my whole body without ever using her hands.

When she was done, she simply put her clothes back on, fixed her makeup, and was gone.

I took my time getting out of Claire's bed. I waited until I was sure I would have her scent on me for the entire day before I got up, sliced myself an onion bagel using an ivory-handled kitchen knife that seemed obscenely expensive for such a mundane task, stuffed

Claire's social security number into my overnight bag, and dressed without showering.

I have five appointments lined up before lunch, and if history repeats itself, two or maybe one will show. Charlie calls it the Jerry Springer Quotient.

"The way I see it," he says, "these people have two options. They can either come here and humiliate themselves by taking typing tests and filing exams or they can sit at home and watch Jerry Springer. Pick your poison."

Charlie is interviewing a black guy with several splotchy tattoos crawling up his arm. I hear Charlie ask the applicant if he has any references besides his parole officer.

The receptionist buzzes me to say that my eleven o'clock appointment has arrived. "Send him back," I say.

He is tall, maybe six feet two inches, with wavy brown hair and a square jaw. He is familiar to me in some way I can't place. Maybe he is a character actor or shops at the same Ralph's that I do. But that's not it. There is something in his face that makes me want to crawl under my desk. Something that says I have felt this way before about this person. We are shaking hands and he is smiling and I am smiling and I am cross-checking his smile with guys who beat me up in elementary school, guys who had sex with my ex-girlfriend, guys who Robert Stack has warned me about on *Unsolved Mysteries*. Nothing comes up. We sit down at my desk.

"Give me a moment to look over your résumé," I say. There it is in bold Times New Roman font: Waiter, Intermezzo. "Oh," I say, "Intermezzo is a nice place."

"Used to be," he says, "but the clientele has changed."

"Is that why you quit?"

"I didn't quit," he says. "I hope this isn't a problem, but I got fired over something really stupid."

I hear Charlie tell his applicant that sometimes prison can be a blessing. Sometimes four walls can make you think more clearly. At that very moment, I hoped Charlie was right, because the walls were creeping toward me again.

"What was that?" I ask.

"Some couple stiffed me on a seven-hundred-dollar dinner," he says. "I couldn't come up with the money so here I am."

"Here you are," I say.

"Here to get my money," he says. The ceiling is falling. The floor is rising. I am being squeezed into a tiny box, but my applicant, Rick Kite, is still large and handsome. He has found me. The charade is over. The police are probably at HealthMerge cuffing Claire.

Fake. Liar. Cheat.

We nod at each other. He knows. Rick Kite is here to collect his bill.

"I don't have it on me," I say, "but I can get it."

He laughs. I undo my tie. He is still laughing. I can feel sweat rolling down my side. Charlie's applicant stands up and shows off an Oakland Raiders tattoo that is etched onto his belly.

"I didn't think you guys handed out money," Rick says. "So I'll take whatever comes along. I'm flexible."

"That's good," I say and manage to force out a grin. "You'll work a lot if you're flexible."

Before I go to HealthMerge, I stop at JCPenney and purchase a new dress shirt since I have sweated through my other. Nothing like the tangible evidence of your misdeeds to get the sweat glands working.

I find Claire's Saab in the visitor parking lot and pull in next to it. It's a good sign: twelve-thirty and she's still working.

The HealthMerge building is several stories high and decorated inside with marble and glass. All of the employees are dressed in suits and have ID cards pinned to their chests. There are computers on every desk and an intercom system pages someone once every minute or so.

There are a thousand conversations happening at once. I listen for trouble.

"We can't offer that program to everyone," a woman says.

"There is a time and a place for this kind of behavior," a man says.

"We need toner on machines six and seven," another woman says.

I take the elevator to the ninth floor. A receptionist sits behind a tall circular desk with a headset on. She sees me and raises a finger for me to be quiet.

"Tell you what, baby," the receptionist says. "You tell them what customers do is not your fault. You can't be watching every move they make, you know what I'm saying? You serve food and you bring drinks. The bill belongs to management."

I'm getting very warm.

"Can I help you?" the receptionist asks after she hangs up.

"Yes," I say. "I'm here from Staff Genius. Just wanted to see how our people were working out."

"What kinda jobs do you get people?" the receptionist asks.

"All kinds," I say.

"Entry level?"

I know where this is going. "Sure."

"Not for me," the receptionist says. "See, my son Bobby thinks he's gonna get fired from his waiting job. Management wants to can him because some Hollywood types ran out on their bill."

"That happens," I say. "People just forget to pay."

"Yeah, well, my son's honest. Why don't you give me your card and I'll have him call you."

"I don't have one with me," I lie. "So just tell him to call and ask for Charlie."

The receptionist takes my number and shows me through the office to where my people are working. I don't see Claire. I see Rosie Klinger staring into space. I see the Thompson sisters, Bonnie and Joan, typing from a dictation machine. I see all of the other secretaries, but I don't see Claire.

The receptionist takes me to a closed office door and knocks. "Mr.

Jennings will want to see you," she says. Mr. Jennings is the manager of the department. We stand there and I'm sure I hear giggling. I'm sure I hear kissing. I'm sure I feel Claire moving behind the door. She is in there. The receptionist knocks again. "Don't know what's taking him," she says, but I do. I'm about to break the door down when it opens and Claire walks out followed by Mr. Jennings.

Claire barely brushes my body with her shoulder. She smells like sex.

She touches me because she touches everyone.

"You must be Lonnie Milton," Mr. Jennings says, extending his hand. I take it and squeeze it as hard as I can, trying to see if I can feel Claire in his touch. Mr. Jennings never stops smiling. "Why don't you come into my office?" he says and closes the door behind me. Claire fills the air.

Mr. Jennings sits behind his desk in a tall, swiveling, leather chair. He is older, maybe fifty, and has an expensive gold watch and probably a tummy tuck. There are pictures on his desk of children and dogs. There is a football encased in glass that says "USC Rose Bowl" on it. He is Corporate.

"You really sent some dynamite people over," Mr. Jennings says.

"We try to find the best candidates for all of our jobs," I say.

"Well, that Claire is fantastic," he says.

"I know," I say.

"Tell me," Mr. Jennings says, "how much would it cost if we wanted to hire her immediately for a full-time job?"

It would cost a pound of your flesh. It would cost you your family. "I'd have to go back to my office and work out the numbers," I say.

Mr. Jennings picks up his phone. "Phyllis, will you send Claire into my office?" He hangs up and starts tapping his desk with a pen. "How about we work out a flat fee," he says. "Something like three thousand."

Claire opens the door. "You asked for me, Bill?"

Bill. She calls him Bill.

"Have a seat," he says.

Claire sits down beside me. She never stops staring at Mr. Jennings.

Bill.

"Claire," Bill says, "we've just been discussing how we'd like to bring you on to the HealthMerge team."

"That's very generous of you," Claire says. She says it quietly, though. She says it with her eyes looking at her feet. She crosses her legs and I see the tan skin of her thigh.

And then there is nothing. Bill is staring at her. I am staring at her. She is staring at the floor.

Here is Bill Jennings: all tanned flesh and corporate America. Perfect teeth. Perfect smile. Never had to fight for anything in his life. Maybe played a little fullback at SC. Maybe married a Tri Delt. Maybe calls his son "Champ" and his daughter "Sugar." Probably coaches soccer on the weekends. Probably supports several local charities. Probably just got done fucking Claire.

"Ten thousand dollars," I say. "Cash." Both Claire and Bill look at me. "Ten thousand dollars and she's all yours, Bill." I can see Claire from the corner of my eye. She is impressed.

The intercom pages Bill Jennings. He says nothing. It pages him again. Claire and I both stand up to leave. "What the hell is going on?" Bill asks.

"If you want Claire," I say and then I can't believe what I'm saying, "then I need ten thousand dollars in cash. That price includes fucking her today and the assurance that I won't go to your son's soccer game and tell him that Dad is cheating on Mom."

Here I am: Lonnie Milton. Junior executive. Dinner thief. Blackmailer. The guy who thinks things through before deciding. The guy who searches the IKEA catalogue for bargains. The guy who will take your job and ruin your family and will never know the meaning of bad karma.

Claire puts her hand on my arm and squeezes.

"I can pay a thousand today," Bill says. "And then more later."

"Fifteen hundred," Claire says and Bill takes out his wallet.

Six

I tell Julie everything. She is thrilled. "Did you meet Bill Jennings?" she asks.

"Yes," I say. "Helluva guy."

"A real sweetheart," Julie says. "I've known him forever."

I hang up with Julie and go to the bathroom. Charlie is smoking a cigarette and staring at himself in the mirror.

"I didn't know you smoked," I say.

"I don't," Charlie says. "I just thought I'd try one on for size." Charlie stubs the cigarette out and strikes an Elvis pose in the mirror. "Thank you very much, Los Angeles, and good night."

"HealthMerge was a real success," I say.

"Good to know," he says. "I'm sure your file will be updated."

"Yeah," I say. My file will now include extorting money from one of the nation's largest health-care providers. "Claire really knocked them out, I guess."

"I wish I had a girlfriend I could whore out to the clients," he says. He isn't looking at me, so he doesn't see my face collapse. "I don't even have a girlfriend," he says, then turns and faces me. "You think Claire might be able to set me up?"

"I'll ask," I say.

"Good, real good," Charlie says, but he's not talking to me. He has another cigarette between his lips and he's making faces into the mirror.

I'm not home for five minutes when my mom calls. She talks while I count out seven one-hundred-dollar bills and one fifty to give to Claire. "Your sister tells me you've got someone in your life."

"Not really," I say. "We're just friends."

"Lonnie," Mom says, "don't get tied up with another woman who sleeps around. There are diseases out there that can kill you."

"I know," I say. "I'm careful."

"I saw a story on *20/20* about a boy who was very careful and got AIDS anyway. Sixteen years old and he might as well be dead."

"You watch too much TV," I say.

"And then there are those two pretty little girls in the Midwest who are connected at the chest. Their parents should have just smothered them at birth."

"Okay, Mom, I gotta go."

"Don't get me started on that Internet," she says and then starts. I set the phone down and pour myself a glass of orange juice. When I get back, she's still talking. I toss in an "uh-huh" just to show her I'm still there.

Long story short, my mom talks about the evils of the Internet for another twenty minutes while I flip through the stations. The Channel 4 news comes on and I watch a guy in a blue Impala race down the freeway with a passel of police officers on his tail.

"I've gotta go, Mom," I say again, "there's a high-speed chase on Channel 4."

"All right," she says. "I'll see you Monday night. Bring Cindy if you want."

"It's Claire," I say and we hang up. The Impala is really moving now, darting in and out of traffic, swerving to avoid other cars. The anchorman narrates the events by saying, "He's really putting some people's lives in jeopardy here," and his female sidekick says, "Yes, Chuck, he is acting very negligent."

I switch to Channel 2, where they have the same footage running but from a slightly different angle. They have an expert in high-speed chases talking about the dynamics of just this sort of thing. He says, "The driver of the Impala must have committed a crime of some great magnitude to warrant this kind of flight."

I click over to Channel 7, and it's the same thing there, too. But then, along the bottom of the screen, a scroll of words spreads out. The Impala races above them, never quite catching the last letter.

But I do. I make out the words very carefully.

CO-WORKERS STUNNED AS MEDICAL EXECUTIVE PLUNGES TO HIS DEATH IN DOWNTOWN HIGH-RISE. DETAILS AFTER THE CHASE.

Cry if you have to, I tell myself. Go ahead and tear up all that money and flush it down the toilet. Stick your head in the oven and inhale gas fumes for a couple minutes. Wish that you contract AIDS or testicular cancer or Alzheimer's.

Evacuate.

Fly to Kosovo.

Go smother two little girls connected at the chest.

Whatever happens, don't go to Claire's. Don't get into the car and drive right now because you're liable to get yourself killed. Just sit here in the living room and watch the chase on a different channel. Maybe make yourself some Top Ramen or order a pizza. Catch a game show.

Just don't get up.

Don't change into those pleated pants. Take that butterfly-collared shirt off. For God's sake, no cologne.

"Don't valet," I say to Claire and hang up the phone.

■ ■ ■

Mistral is slow for a Friday night, so I get a table by the window. One of the Lakers is sitting behind me, his long legs sticking into the aisle. I comment to him that he is a real hazard for the waiters, and we both share a laugh. He tells me that he saw me the other night at Sky Bar and that my girl is very pretty. I have never been to Sky Bar in my life. I thank him anyway.

Claire arrives just as the basketball player is leaving. He gives me a thumbs-up.

"Friend of yours?" Claire asks.

"Is now," I say.

A waiter comes by and Claire orders a glass of merlot. She is wearing a tight black dress and her hair is pulled back away from her face. I reach my hand across the table and Claire takes it. "We need to talk," I say.

"Yes," she says. "I need your advice on a new home I'm purchasing."

"No," I say.

Claire's wine arrives and she sips at it without letting go of my hand. "Jake," she says, using my fake name, "this is not the place."

"But it is," I say. It is the only place where I feel disconnected from my own actions. The only place where I'm not responsible anymore.

"I saw the news, if that's what you mean."

"What are we going to do?"

"We keep on living," Claire says. She tightens her grip on my hand, then leans toward me. "He would have died anyway. A heart attack, probably. Or drunk driving. He was an accident waiting for the right point of impact."

"He had kids, Claire."

She lets go of my hand, downs the rest of her wine, and then shakes her empty glass in the air. The waiter comes and refills it. "You told me that sort of thing doesn't bother you," she says. "So what if he gets in the way, you have bills to pay."

Claire sips at her wine. She knows my holes.

I've never seen a dead person. I've never gone days without sleep. I've never prayed for anything I couldn't afford to buy.

Claire isn't wearing any jewelry tonight. No watch. No earrings. Her only accessory tonight is me. I make for a lovely complement to any outfit.

"I'm not a parasite," I say.

Claire orders duck salad. I order a plate of noodles with no sauce. We don't speak during dinner. Other people walk by our table and say hello. Tell us how well we look. Tell us they hope we come to their party. One woman walks up, kisses me on the cheek, touches my back with her hand, and tells me she has heard great things about my production company.

Fake. Liar. Cheat.

"Aren't you quite the star," Claire says. We have just ordered dessert, although I feel like someone has replaced my stomach with ball bearings. I slide an envelope across the table. Claire picks it up, counts the money, and stuffs it into her purse. "I didn't sleep with him," she says, "if you're wondering."

We argue in Mistral.

We argue in a cab that drives up and down Ventura Boulevard.

We argue in front of her convertible Saab.

Some people can manipulate you. Some can twist your words around as if they're working for the government. Some can tell you to buy a toothbrush and then change your entire world.

The long and the short: She smiled at him. She insinuated that she might like to take her clothes off for him sometime. She touched him. Not touched him touched him, but enough. I know about this. She went into his office with a cup of coffee and made idle chitchat about cheating on his wife.

"Because I don't know how to type," she says to me. "Because I didn't want to get you in trouble. This is your problem, Lonnie, not mine." We are standing beside her car when she says this. I want to do something that will make her think I'm dangerous, make her think I am in control of this situation. I kick her car door and leave a sizable dent. "What are you doing?" Claire shouts. She is angrier than I have ever seen her. "This isn't even mine."

My foot is numb. In a moment it will hurt a great deal.

"Yes, it is," I say. "That's your jacket in the backseat."

"I don't own it, Lonnie."

Two police cars race down Ventura, sirens blaring. We are about a mile away from Mistral, but when the cops come to a halt, I have a pretty good idea where they are.

I should have had sauce with my noodles.

"Is it leased?"

Claire reaches into her purse and pulls out the envelope I gave her at dinner. She counts the money again. "Give me another three hundred," she says. "It's going to cost at least a thousand to get this fixed."

When I hand her the money, she shoves it into her wallet and climbs into her car.

"So that's it?" I ask. "You're just going home?"

It's summer, so when Claire punches her Saab into drive and screeches away from the curb, the breeze actually feels nice.

Seven

I wake up Saturday morning and everything is normal. The TV is still on. There is a carton of rocky road ice cream melting on my nightstand. It is 9 A.M. and the sun is flooding my bedroom.

I close my eyes and try to remember my dream. It had something to do with some guy jumping out of a window. Some Los Angeles Laker thinks he knows me. A beautiful woman makes me kick a car door.

When I roll over onto my stomach and my foot decides to stay in its same painful place, it hits me.

These things happened. Welcome to the real world, Lonnie.

I pull the covers back and take a look at my foot. At least two of my toes are broken. I know this because they are completely black and very swollen. My entire foot is swollen, really. I get out of bed and hop into my kitchen for some ice. There is none. I snatch a bag of frozen peas out of the freezer and stick my foot into it.

I need to figure this all out. I need to diagram this situation and make rational sense out of it. Simple algebra. I meet Claire. We steal a few meals. We tell a few lies. I fall in love, or lust, or whatever. We have sex. I extort a bunch of money from some guy I don't know. He kills himself. I break my foot.

These satellites swirling around my sun just keep colliding. If I can recover just one of them, maybe I can figure out how everything began to spin.

There are three messages on my answering machine. Two are from Visa wondering where my payment is and one is from Charlie. It's from last night. He is probably in a bar somewhere calling to say how drunk he is.

"Lonnie, man, I'm pretty ripped up right now. I just had to call and tell you. Look, man, I don't know how to say this, but I think your girl is here with some Persian guy. I dunno, man, cuz these Jager shots got me pretty dulled, but I think it's her. So, you know, I wanted to let you know before you found out on *Hard Copy* or something. Call me or whatever," Charlie says before the operator comes on and tells him it's forty cents more for the next three minutes and then there is nothing.

Charlie makes the most sense when he speaks in epigrams, but I still feel something hollow fill up my stomach.

You wake up one morning in your own bed and nothing fits.

You wake up one morning in a mansion in Brentwood and you don't ask any questions. You don't ask about her living arrangements. You don't ask why she doesn't work.

You wake up one morning and you've killed a man.

This is how I met Claire Gooden. Big blank slate. Some people aren't smart enough to hold down real jobs, I say to everyone. Some people just don't interview well.

Some people dance cheek to cheek, my eighth-grade modern-dance instructor said on the first day of school. I never knew what that meant until right now.

There is a knock on my front door. I hobble over to the peephole and look out. My next-door neighbor, an elderly woman named Ann, stares back at me. "Sorry to bother," she says when I open the door, "but do you use your coupons?" I look down and she has my *L.A. Times* in her hands.

"No," I say. "You can have them." Ann starts tearing at my paper looking for coupons, handing it back to me in dismantled sections. "I think they come on Sundays, don't they?"

Ann stops and gives me a look of utter shock. "You didn't hear the news?"

You wake up and the *L.A. Times* is out of business?

"Today they have a special restaurant coupon section," Ann says. "To quell the crime, you know."

I give Ann the entire newspaper and tell her she can have tomorrow's, too.

I understand myself to be fairly normal. But there is something about all of this that makes me excited. Makes me feel like this is a position in my life that I will say was good; that I'll make these little mistakes work for me. Claire is a woman I might be able to change.

My whole body feels like an Indian burn. Like someone has twisted all of my skin into tight strips and if they move just an inch I might tear away. I took psychology in college so I know something about the dark side of competition. I know that friendly murder takes place in business, sports, all relationships. To earn a point. To defeat an opponent.

So when I turn on the TV and see a videotape of Bill Jennings tumbling in slow motion from the top story of the HealthMerge facility, I'm not shocked.

"This is not my skin," I say, then pinch myself to prove it. I say it again and again until the words mean absolutely nothing and I have a bruise in the shape of West Virginia on my thigh.

All that registers are three words: Fake. Liar. Cheat.

She calls when I am in the shower. Her message makes us sound like we are a nice suburban couple. "Hi, Lonnie, it's me. You're probably in the bathroom or something. Call me when you get back."

A towel is wrapped around my waist and my foot is in a bag of frozen hash browns when I call her back. She answers on the first ring.

"Sorry about last night," Claire says. "I went a little crazy."

"Charlie said he saw you at some bar," I say.

"That's possible." A police siren screams past my apartment building and I freeze for a moment. "You still there, Lonnie?"

"Yes," I say.

"Look," Claire says. "Maybe we should slow things down. I see how jumpy you are getting."

"I keep seeing myself on the news," I say.

"No, you don't," Claire says.

It's not like watching a baseball game and imagining yourself being the first baseman for the Oakland A's. That is nearly impossible. But when I see Bill Jennings falling or coupons for free dinners in my paper, I see myself very clearly.

"Maybe we should talk somewhere," I say.

"We're talking right now."

"I'd like to see you," I say. "Try to sort everything out."

Claire sighs. "Tell me about your family."

"Claire," I start, but she interrupts me.

"Tell me about your family, Lonnie. It will help."

I tell her that I knew my father for four, maybe five years. There are pictures that document the first day we met but nothing significant marks the final departure. My parents were married for eleven years and now have been divorced almost twice as long. His name is Hugh and he lives somewhere in the Northwest.

"You don't speak?" Claire asks.

"Never," I say.

"So you were raised by your mother?"

"Yes," I say and wonder where all of this is taking me. Behind Claire's voice I hear a television set running cartoons.

"Men need to be raised by men," Claire says. "Gives them a better sense of who they are."

"I think you're wrong," I say and Claire laughs.

"Who teaches a painter how to paint? Not a florist."

My mother wrote the first infomercials, mostly for Time-Life products, then later for bizarre exercise and skin-care devices. My sister thinks she may have had an affair with that guy from Ronco.

"So do you think you have the franchise on dysfunctional?" Claire asks.

"What is this, Claire?" The cartoons behind Claire switch off. The hash browns have melted so I open up the freezer and find a Swanson's TV dinner to put my foot into.

"I'm just trying to get a handle on things," Claire says.

Since Claire appeared in my life, I've been able to nail down everything else around me, save for her. I'm on the fast track to middle management at Staff Genius. I'm doing things that make me feel dangerous, alive. When I wake up in the morning, I don't debate for ten minutes whether it's going to be a Pop-Tart or Cap'n Crunch. I just eat.

Claire solved nothing for me nor did she offer a better understanding of the world. But she gave me this skin. This place where nothing else was quite as significant.

"This whole thing with us," Claire says, "is fun, isn't it? We have fun together, don't we, Lonnie?"

"Yes," I say, because it is. Or was. Or will be.

"You just raised the bar yesterday. I knew you would, too. I want to be comfortable with you, Lonnie. No more secrets."

No more secrets. I never had any.

"Let's start fresh," she says. "I mean, let's go bowling or something and be friends in the real world."

The apple crumb dessert in my Swanson's TV dinner ice pack is starting to get gooey. I pull my foot from the box and it is still swollen and the color of several melted crayons.

"I think I need to go to the hospital," I say.

"I'll come get you," Claire says.

Two hours and a sizable amount of Vicodin later, a doctor tells me I have four broken toes and a chipped bone along the side of my foot.

"We call it a soccer-boyfriend break," the doctor says. "Was it a person or an object?"

"The door had it coming," I say.

"Well," the doctor says, "keep kicking doors and you're not going to have a girlfriend."

"Do I need a cast?"

"Yes," the doctor says, "but just a soft one. We'll put you into a boot and you'll be fine."

Before the doctor is through wrapping my foot, his pager goes off. "This isn't like TV," the doctor says, dialing the number on his beeper. "The interesting things happen all day long."

"Must be fun," I say, but he is listening to someone on the line. When he hangs up he looks frustrated.

"Never understood why people commit suicide," the doctor says. "All it does is make other people miserable."

"I agree," I say as a shard of pain drifts through the Vicodin.

"Did you see that guy who jumped off the high-rise yesterday?"

"No," I say. No, I did not see him. No, I don't know why he would do such a thing.

"No matter how far down the bottom is, I think you can climb up. Don't you?"

I nod my head.

"Anyway," the doctor says and continues to wrap my foot in silence.

I can hear the sound of an approaching ambulance and wonder what kind of wounded person is in it. It's the Vicodin, I tell myself. Think about something else.

"That for you?" I ask.

"Eventually," the doctor says.

I watch all the medical shows. I know all the ER horror stories. Maybe it's an actor with a sucking chest wound. Maybe some aspiring model is suffering from bradycardia because of extreme fear of the runway.

"Do you want to check?"

"We're almost done here," the doctor says.

There is a rush of activity outside the exam room I am in. I hear someone call out for a crash cart.

My mother always wanted me to be a doctor. Or a dentist. Or a lawyer. My mother never suggested that I might like temporary placement as a career. Not once in high school did someone say that their lifelong dream was to someday find three legal word processors for a large downtown firm.

"Do you get many subdural hematomas?"

The doctor doesn't look up. "Mostly on Friday nights," he says.

I'm still not sure what a word processor does. Do they slice? Do they dice? Do they make julienne fries?

"People like to get drunk and fight," the doctor says.

Charlie says this, too. He says this phenomenon is caused by health insurance. "People figure, What the fuck, I've got insurance. Let's get it on."

"Okay," the doctor says. "You're all set." My foot is wrapped in a soft cast and I have been fitted with an open-toed boot that makes me walk like Frankenstein. "Have you got a ride home?"

"Yes," I say. "My girlfriend is here."

"Good," the doctor says and writes me out a prescription for more Vicodin. "Take these for the pain. Come back in two weeks and we'll make sure everything is healing."

I walk out of the exam room and am nearly run over by two orderlies pushing a gurney. There is a child on the gurney, its head split open down the front. I don't know if it's a boy or a girl.

Moments later, another gurney is rushed by me. This time the body is an adult woman. I know this only because I see that her fingernails are long and painted.

"What happened?" I ask the desk clerk.

"Lady drove her kids off a cliff," the clerk says. "Some kinda suicide pact."

"I can't believe that," I say.

"Happens all the time," the clerk says.

■ ■ ■

Claire is asleep in the waiting room. There is a very fat man wearing a Hawaiian shirt sitting next to her. He is staring down her top. I sit across from him. He nods at me in the way men nod at each other when they don't want to seem obscenely obvious.

"What happened to your foot?" Mr. Heavy asks.

"Attacked by a pit bull."

Mr. Heavy shakes his index finger at me. "I'll tell you what," he says. "Meanest sons of bitches in the whole animal kingdom."

Claire stirs in her chair, her top gaping a little further. Mr. Heavy takes an exaggerated look. "You gotta check this business out," he says to me. I go and sit on the other side of Claire.

I lean over and take a quick glance at the view.

"I ain't kidding," Mr. Heavy says.

"How much if I kiss her on the lips?"

Mr. Heavy reaches into his pocket and pulls out a crumpled wad of bills. "Whatever I got," he says. I lean over and brush her lips with mine. Her tongue forces its way between my lips and the next thing I know, she is climbing on top of me.

In the car, I count the money. It is a little more than a hundred dollars. "We have enough for dinner and a movie," I say. We are driving through Reseda with the top down on the Saab. It is hot, at least 100 degrees, and the smog makes my skin feel gritty. Claire is done up like Jackie O today. The white scarf she wears over her hair makes me feel like I'm in an old James Dean movie.

James Dean never had to wear a sissy-looking boot on his broken foot.

"I'm not free tonight," Claire says. "Or Sunday, really."

"What about your new resolve?" I say.

"I need to fix some things, Lonnie."

There are questions I need to ask her. This I know. There is a history lesson in Claire that needs my immediate attention. But she smiles at me.

She takes my hand in hers while we drive and I think that these questions can wait until she's free. We can sit down and pretend we're in a scene from *The Big Chill* or *The Breakfast Club* and just *talk*.

We stop for a red light at the intersection of Reseda and Ventura. A Jetta pulls beside us. A woman sits alone in the front seat, the windows rolled up against the heat. Her hair is being blown by the expensive nonfactory air. She looks at me and frowns.

Here is a perfect little couple, she is probably thinking. I bet they worry about the ozone. Maybe they recycle. They make a combined annual income of just over $100,000. They go to revolving pot-luck dinners and always prepare something exciting.

It's the Vicodin.

They eat eggplant because it's good for you. They vote for city council because people do make a difference. Maybe they smoke a little pot now and then, but who doesn't?

Before the light changes, I frown back at her. It will give her something to think about while she's in traffic.

Claire drops me off at my apartment but doesn't come in. "Call me on Sunday," she says and kisses me gently on the cheek.

"I will," I say, but I don't get out of the car. I want to say something, anything really, that will make Claire just open up. "I know this sounds weird," I say, "but my mom is coming into town Monday night. I'd like it if you came to dinner with us."

Claire takes a deep breath and nods her head twice. "If it's important to you," she says and I tell her it is. "Then all right."

It isn't until after Claire has driven off that I notice the police car parked in front of my building. If you live in a large apartment complex, seeing the police is somewhat commonplace. Either someone's car has been robbed or someone is being evicted.

So I don't pay much attention, either, to the large pile of clothes strewn over the front lawn. People in apartments find new and interesting ways to fight all the time.

I take the elevator up to the third floor. On the second floor, the doors open and Ann, my neighbor, steps in. I smile at her because I smile at everyone.

"Terrible thing," Ann says.

"Yes," I say.

"Have the police found any clues?"

"It was the butler in the den with a kitchen knife," I say.

"Good that you can keep your sense of humor about you," Ann says. "I'm about ready to give my notice."

The elevator opens and I hear it before I see it. The cackle of police radios, the laughter of people who don't give a shit about something. People saying things like "10-4" and "Roger that."

This is a big deal.

The door to my apartment is missing. For that matter, so are both of my couches. My Zenith TV. My microwave. Most of my clothes—except for the ones on the front lawn. A jar of Skippy peanut butter. All of my compact discs. Two flank steaks and a London broil. In short, everything but the kitchen sink.

"The way I see it," Officer Kenny says after I have stopped screaming, "someone wanted to send you a message."

"Probably because you play your TV so damn loud," Glen the building manager says. "I told you, Lonnie, people have been complaining."

My foot is throbbing. My head is throbbing.

"I'm not surprised, really," Glen says.

They have left me the following items: my answering machine, a tube of hair gel, a box of Ding Dongs, my Nintendo 64, my computer, one of my phones, a drawer full of ugly sweaters my grandmother gave me, a picture of my ex-girlfriend Sherry, three Jackie Chan films, and $400 in large bills that I extorted from Bill Jennings just prior to his unfortunate departure from the world.

"And you didn't happen to hear anyone removing my door?" I ask Glen.

"I don't get paid enough to listen," Glen says. "I'm not even supposed to be here today."

After I punch Glen in the face, I make it a point to also kick him with my sissy Frankenstein boot.

Eight

Charlie is kind enough to post bail for me. The police wouldn't let me bring my Vicodin into the holding cell, so when I get into Charlie's car I gobble two down like they are M&M's.

"Man," Charlie says, "I think it's time you started going to some kind of support group."

"I'm fine."

"Anger management or something."

"I'm fine."

"My cousin Billy," Charlie says, "he got five years for pushing steroids on the street. He started a support group for drug dealers, maybe he's got some contacts."

"I'm fine," I say, and Charlie gets the hint that I don't want to talk. For five minutes, Charlie is actually quiet as he negotiates the traffic on the 101.

"So what's up with your apartment?"

"I have a good feeling it's not mine anymore," I say.

"Are you going to stay with Claire?"

"We're hardly even dating," I say.

"I'll say," Charlie says. "She's bad news, man. You got my message, right?"

"Yes."

"I was at Dragonfly with my boy Dale from Equifax and she comes sashaying up to the bar like some kinda supermodel," Charlie says. My foot is starting to feel warm. Pins and needles start pushing through my palms. It's the Vicodin.

"So I'm like, whoa, that's Lonnie's girl, so I don't make any overt plays in her direction."

"A true gentleman," I say. I'm starting to sweat. I read the directions on the prescription bottle. Take with food. The last food I ingested was a carton of rocky road ice cream some eighteen hours previous. My stomach starts to hurt.

"Then I see the Sheik of Araby walk up behind her and plant one on her neck. I'm thinking, okay, it's on. I was willing to fight for your girl's honor," Charlie says. I roll down the window to get some fresh air. What I end up with is a mouthful of diesel exhaust from the semi in front of us. Charlie doesn't notice that I'm suffering, so he continues.

"So I pop another Jager shot down, you know, to get pumped up for a holy war with this crazy Shiite, when Claire turns around and sticks her tongue in his mouth. Man, I nearly lost it right there. Dale had to practically tie my ass to the bar for the rest of the night."

When we eventually pass the semi, I try to gobble up some clean air. My stomach is Mary Lou Retton. My stomach is a tornado. My stomach is the battle for the Gaza Strip.

"Oh, shit," Charlie says. "Why didn't you say something, I would have pulled over."

My stomach is on the floor of Charlie's 1994 Ford Mustang.

"Man," Charlie says, "you've gotta let your anger out before it leads to physical illness. I'm gonna give you my cousin's phone number."

Taped to my new front door is an eviction notice. There are some things you can still count on.

"Damn," Charlie says.

I have seven new messages on my answering machine. Three are from Glen, my now former apartment manager, threatening me with great bodily harm and severe civil liability. He closes his final message by reminding me that his sister is a lawyer and that he will own me.

According to Charlie, the actual worth of all the trace elements in my body is only about three dollars.

There are two messages from my mother regarding her impending arrival in Los Angeles, one from my sister, Karen, who claims to have a pop-culture trivia question to stump me with, and the obligatory message from Visa.

One of my neighbors, probably Ann, brought my clothes up from the front lawn and folded them nicely. I pick through them to see if there is anything worth keeping.

I hear Charlie rummaging around in the kitchen. "Oh, man," he says, and I think, What now?

"These are some coldhearted bastards," Charlie says when he walks into my bedroom holding the frozen Swanson's dinner I used as an ice pack. "They ate your dessert and just left the chicken and the corn to rot."

That was today, I think. A few hours ago, I had two couches from IKEA that looked splendid with the Pottery Barn coffee table I also no longer possess. My life, while spiraling in an uncertain direction, still had a certain locus, a physical center where I could try and work things out. No matter the cause of these problems I was having—and I hesitate to call them problems, more like difficult moral humps—at least I knew which remote control operated the TV, which drawer my socks were in, and how many clean hand towels I had.

Charlie picks up a shirt from the pile and examines it. "Hey," he says, "this is mine."

I look at it closely and then I remember. The cool feel of the silk on my chest. The way Claire touched my hand across the table on our first date at Intermezzo. That way she made me feel: in control, but still spinning in her little web. Confident, like I could say anything or do anything and it would be right. It would be exciting and sexy.

"It's out of style," I say.

"I paid fifty bucks for it. Anything that costs fifty bucks can't be out of style. This shirt is a magnet." Charlie folds his shirt carefully and takes it back into the kitchen.

They've stolen my autographed Oakland A's baseball. It had sat in a plastic case for eighteen years. It outlasted Jimmy Carter, Ronald Reagan, and George Bush. I never played with it. I never let Scott Sorenson, my next-door neighbor growing up, touch it. For years I kept it in a sealed box thinking that the light of day would harm it.

It outlasted *M*A*S*H, Eight Is Enough, Sanford and Son, Manimal,* and *Battlestar Galactica.* It even outlasted *Seinfeld.*

There is nothing hot or sexy or electric about this. I can't find a simple answer for why this has happened to me. No one who knows me hates me this much. I don't have many close friends because I suffer stupidity so poorly and likewise with enemies.

And this issue of karma is moot. No one knows me well enough to steal my front door and my couches, much less care about how I spend my evenings. I did mean to give Charlie his shirt back.

I call my sister, Karen, from Charlie's apartment.

"Sounds like some kind of strange cult or something," Karen says. "You know, like Heaven's Gate or that Kool-Aid thing in the seventies. Stealing someone's front door and couch is like saying you're not welcome to tread on this planet."

"They stole my IKEA couches, Karen. There is nothing remotely metaphysical about that."

There is a pause on the line while Karen considers this. Having a degree in religious studies and a job as a bank manager makes your mind work in odd ways. "I don't know," she says finally, "this whole millennium business has people really trying to debunk the capitalistic society. Maybe by stealing your couches they are making a statement about the world's comfort level."

I don't respond to Karen because I don't think I want to play this game anymore. After about thirty seconds of dead silence, she starts up again in a different direction, her train having been derailed for the time being.

"Anyway, do you need a place to stay?" she asks.

"I'm going to shack up with Charlie for tonight at least. Then I've gotta find a new place."

I hadn't mentioned that I punched my landlord in the face, so I had to explain that, too. It gave Karen an information overload.

"Do you still have a job?"

"Yes," I say. Sure. Absolutely. Big promotion coming up. My own office. We'll be offering racketeering services at a discount rate.

"I'll call you on Monday then," she says. "I wouldn't tell Mom until dinner about all of this. She'll be pissed."

"I'm an adult," I say. "This is not something she can be mad at me for."

"You never leave the nest," Karen says.

Charlie is in his kitchen frying me an egg, so I sit on his couch with my foot elevated on top of two pillows. I've swallowed enough Vicodin for one day, so I decide to let my foot throb.

On the floor in front of me is the futon Charlie has set up for me to sleep on. The mattress is about an inch thick. Not quite Claire's four-poster bed. Folded on the carpet is a set of *Star Wars* sheets that I am supposed to use. I can smell bacon. Charlie says something about hash browns.

I get up from the couch and find my bottle of pain pills in the bathroom.

"Let's go out to dinner," I say. "My treat."

I don't dress up because nothing seems to look good with my swollen foot inside the sissy boot. Charlie takes great care with his hair. He slicks it back using two different brands of gel, but nothing makes him happy. He spikes it all straight up. Then he combs it like Caesar, and finally settles for a Los Angeles Lakers cap.

I know this is stupid, but I'm looking for Claire.

Instead of sitting at Charlie's trying to figure out my little quandaries, I'm looking for one of them. Instead of keeping weight off of my foot, I'm balancing very closely just over the third rail.

"Fuck it," Charlie says.

We go to the Opium Den and have drinks. She's not there.

We go to Dragonfly and she's not there. I have two shots of vodka and I smoke a cigar. A woman tells me she wants me to help her with a very large land purchase. We talk about land in Calabasas. I share some insight into the increasing market values in the Silverlake area. I tell her to call me at the office. She nods and smiles, and Charlie looks at me like I'm Charles Manson.

"What was that?" he asks.

"Must have thought I was someone else."

"I don't know," he says. "You seemed to know what she was talking about."

We drive to Santa Monica to shoot pool at Gotham Hall. The place is stocked with Middle Eastern men wearing vests with no shirt.

"Welcome to the Fertile Crescent," Charlie says.

I don't see Claire. But this isn't her crowd.

"There's that guy," Charlie says, pointing across the room. We are both very drunk. It is twelve-thirty.

Sitting on a barstool is a dark-complexioned man of maybe thirty-five. He has a mustache and long sideburns. His hair is thinning, but he wears a ponytail. He is not wearing a vest. Instead, he has a butterfly-collared white silk shirt. He is not wearing socks.

Claire floats across the room. Her hair is done differently. Her makeup is flashier. I see other men staring at her. A kid with three Greek letters plastered on his chest tries to intercept her. She brushes her hand across his chest, smiles, and never stops floating.

"Let's go," Charlie says. "Fuck this."

The demonstration continues. I don't know if she can see me.

When she reaches the table, the dark man takes her by the hand and kisses her gently on the cheek. He keeps his eyes open. He sees everyone watching him. That must be a fabulous feeling, living in the center of the world's attention.

When our eyes meet, I nod to him.

Claire pulls away from his embrace and sits down beside him.

"This is torture," Charlie says.

Claire is wearing thick gold earrings. There is a band of gold around her neck. She looks like Cleopatra. Her dress dips forever. It is black and long, but her arms and chest and back are free. I think I see the triangle of moles she has just under her clavicle, but I know that must be impossible. I slip a Vicodin into my mouth and wash it down with some Scotch.

"Are you trying to OD?" Charlie asks.

Claire is the fake. Claire is the liar. Claire is the cheat.

She drapes her arm over his shoulder.

There are so many acts of commonplace terror in the world today that no one would notice if I went outside, grabbed a Glock from some passing gangster, and blew away everyone in this club. I'd get one minute on the local news and a three-picture movie deal. Maybe Johnny Depp would play me alongside Jennifer Jason Leigh as Claire and Scott Baio as Charlie.

It's the Vicodin, however many I have taken.

"You all right?" Charlie says. He is touching my face.

This morning when Claire picked me up at my apartment, she kissed me on the lips in a friendly way. She sat down on my IKEA couch across from my Pottery Barn table and drank a glass of orange juice. I think she might have flipped through *Vanity Fair*. She held my hand as we walked into the hospital. I can remember the proof; she is human.

"Okay," Charlie says. "Stay up."

I am very warm. I am very soft. I am colliding with the air.

The things Claire said to me today: *I need two days. The real world. I'm not available. We have fun. No more secrets.*

"Oh, shit," Charlie says. He is above me. I am flat on my back. There is a growing circle of people around me. I hear Claire.

"Just some drunk," she says.

After they get done pumping my stomach, I feel pretty good. The hospital sends a psychiatrist down to talk with me after my sister tells them I have always cried out for attention.

"Have you been depressed recently?" the shrink asks. The shrink is a woman named June.

"No," I say.

"His house got robbed," Karen says. "He is in a very vulnerable state." I make a mental note to remove my sister as my emergency contact.

Luckily, it is pushing three in the morning, so June the shrink makes hasty work of me. "I don't think your brother was trying to kill himself," she says to my sister. "I do think he needs to get some rest and lay off the painkillers. It's not as if your spleen's been removed, Lonnie. One Vicodin should get you through the whole day. You don't need to go overboard."

When June leaves, Karen hits me on the arm like we are kids again. "What's in your head?" she asks and before I can answer she hits me again. "Nothing!"

Karen has a hickey on her neck.

"You have a hickey," I say.

"I was on a date when the insurance company paged me, you jerk," Karen says.

I see that her eyes have welled up. She is concerned for me. When we were kids, Karen liked to paint my nails and put makeup on me. She got a pretty good laugh from it. I was too young to give a damn at the time, but she has since confided in me that it has placed a large amount of guilt on her shoulders.

"I'm sorry I scared you," I say.

Karen looks around the room. "Can I smoke in here?" she asks.

"I don't see why not," I say.

Karen lights a cigarette and starts pacing back and forth in front of me. Her eyes are just slits. I've seen this look before. The first time was after I told her boyfriend that she was on the phone all night with another boy. I was ten.

"This has gotta stop," Karen says. "Charlie told me all about this crazy girl you're dating."

"We're not dating," I say. Karen waves me off.

"Look at you," she says. "They pumped enough drugs out of your stomach to start a pharmacy."

"My foot hurt," I say.

Karen tosses her cigarette onto the floor and stubs it out with her foot. "Whatever," she says. "Just stop fucking up. No one is worth this."

"I'm bringing her to dinner," I say, although I don't know if I believe that anymore.

"Okay, Lonnie," Karen says, "don't listen to me. Don't listen to your friends. Just go put yourself on an island and act like a native."

Nine

After Karen stormed out of the hospital, I realized two things: I didn't have a ride and I was very hungry. I take a cab to Denny's so I can get something to eat.

I order the Moons Over My Hammy because it sounds good and because I am in a mood where something called Moons Over My Hammy might just cheer me up. It is almost four in the morning, so the normal Denny's customer has been replaced with staggering drunks and high school kids.

So this is bottom. Denny's at four in the morning. Foot in a cast and boot. Stomach purged of painkillers. Moons Over My Hammy cooking on the skillet.

The waitress pours me a cup of coffee and I smile at her. She isn't ugly. The odd yellow glow of the restaurant mutes her features some, but I can see that somewhere under the heavy eye shadow and powder lurks a relatively attractive person.

"What's your name?" I ask.

The waitress points to her nametag without speaking. It says "Hazel." It must be a joke.

"That's a joke, right?" I say.

"No," she says.

"Listen," I say, although I don't know what it is I want her to hear. Hazel leans over the counter and puts her elbows in front of me. "I work for a company," I start to say and Hazel's eyes widen.

This is Los Angeles. Everyone is running some kind of game. So who needs a razor of doubt? Who needs to say the things that don't come true? I'll give out an ounce of hope and maybe things will start running in the right direction.

"A production company, actually. I own it."

Hazel is smiling.

"I think you have what it takes, Hazel," I say. "I think you need to get out of this job, put on a nice dress, and become a star."

"This isn't some kind of come-on or something, is it?" Hazel says.

"No," I say. I take a napkin and write down my fake name. "You call CAA and William Morris and let them know I am interested in you and have them call me if they have any questions."

Hazel takes the napkin and nibbles on the corner of it. "Do you really think I have it?" she asks.

I am a fake. I am a liar. I am a cheat. I make dreams come true.

"You're electric," I say.

My Moons Over My Hammy are delicious and when I am finished with them, Hazel brings me a hot-fudge sundae.

"On the house," she says.

I wake up Charlie by pounding on his front door for twenty minutes. He mumbles something about being worried sick and then tumbles back into bed.

I fix up the futon with the *Star Wars* sheets and lie down. Charlie's VCR blinks 12:00, but I know it is about five in the morning. I am wide awake.

Claire must be worried. I know she saw me. She told me to let her be for two days and I just couldn't.

I get up and call my answering machine. There are two messages. The first is from Julie, my boss. She is crying.

"Bill was such a good friend and a wonderful father," Julie is saying.

This is not happening.

"I don't want to go alone, and Corporate wants us to have a strong presence there," Julie says.

This is like an infomercial for ulcers. Not only does he have one—he makes them, too!

"Why don't we meet in front of Forest Lawn tomorrow at eleven. If you could pick up some flowers, I'd appreciate it. I just can't bring myself to leave the house right now."

There is a beep and Julie's message ends.

Meet Lonnie's Ulcer on Sunday at Forest Lawn Cemetery for a free sample!

"What were you thinking," Claire is whispering as my next message plays. "God, I hope you're all right. I'll try to call you tomorrow," she says, then there is nothing but dead air. She hasn't hung up the phone correctly. I hear someone cough.

Then it begins. It is quiet at first, just slight, moist noises. Then I hear breathing. Heavy breathing. A man's voice that says things I can't hear, won't hear, never want to hear again.

I've never been voyeuristic. I've never watched much pornography. I've always thought that what goes on in the bedroom was made for the bedroom.

But I listen to the tape. I listen for twenty-three minutes, hit the star key on the phone, and listen again.

Charlie lets me wear one of his suits since all of mine have been stolen. I wear one slip-on dress shoe and my cast covered in a dark blue sock.

"You look like a pimp," Charlie says. I choose not to remind him that I am wearing his clothes.

Driving my five-speed Tercel is difficult with my foot, so Charlie lets me borrow his Mustang on the condition that I don't speed and that I don't take any Vicodin.

Charlie has a souped-up Mustang that can hit 150 miles per hour on a straightaway.

My foot is killing me.

"No problem," I tell Charlie.

With the windows down, the Mustang encounters more drag than it should going 115, but it's hot outside and the Vicodin makes everything feel smooth. I crank up the stereo to muffle the sound of the engine.

None of it works. I'm going to a funeral for a man I may have killed.

My boss is standing next to her yellow Honda Prelude in front of Forest Lawn Cemetery. She is wearing a tight black dress that makes her sides ripple. She is sweating and smoking—a combination I have never understood.

"What happened to your foot?" Julie asks when I get out of the car.

"I got mad and kicked a door," I say.

Julie nods her head as if that's something I do every day. I hand her the bundle of flowers I picked up from Conroy's and she smells them. "These are beautiful," she says, then takes a dramatic drag from her cigarette. I am pouring sweat.

"Is the service indoors?" I ask.

"The first half, I'm sure," Julie says.

The chapel is large and simple, save for the twelve-foot Jesus that hangs in the air above the pulpit. Before we take our seats, Julie guides me through the crowd to shake hands with people she says will help me get the Encino office off the ground.

"He's the CFO of Chef Guatemala in Chatsworth," Julie says, pointing to an overweight white man in an expensive suit. "He'll have some light-industrial needs and maybe some accounting business toward the end of each quarter."

We shake hands with the CFO of Chef Guatemala and he tells me how great a guy Bill Jennings was and that he was a scratch golfer.

"Call me in December," he says after Julie informs him that I will be running the Valley branch of Staff Genius. "I'll take you on a tour of the factory. You like burritos?"

"As much as the next guy," I say.

"Great," he says. "I'll get you fixed up with a crate of our products. You'll love 'em."

I have similar conversations with the human resources director for Great Mulching of America, a VP from Kimron Nuedle Outdoor Advertising, an executive from Care California, and someone Julie described as "a big pink gun in the home-security industry."

I do all of this with Jesus staring me down from the rafters and Bill Jennings's open casket about twenty feet from me.

We sit toward the back of the chapel next to a man about Bill's age wearing a tight blue suit and sporting a fraternity pin on his lapel. He keeps blowing his nose and muttering things under his breath.

"Damn," Old Fraternity Guy says.

"The chain will never be broken," he says.

"Here's to the brothers of Sigma, here's to the fellows of Phi," he says and then just says "damn" again.

Julie has the Bible open on her lap.

Here comes the family down the center of the church.

"You had a heart made of chrome," Old Fraternity Guy says.

Here comes the wife. I remember her from the pictures on his desk.

"I need a cigarette," Julie says.

The son has wispy blond hair and looks like a little man in his tailored suit. The daughter has a big nose. Cosmetic surgery will fix that and she will be stunning.

"Damn," he says.

Here comes I'm sick to my stomach.

Here comes Jesus floating over the church like Michael Jordan.

"I am the alpha and the omega," the minister begins.

My mom never made me go to church. I remember one afternoon she and Karen sat me down to explain to me that religion was not something to be forced into. "I was raised a Baptist," Mom said. "It didn't have an effect on me one way or the other. If you want to learn about a particular religion, I'll buy you any book you want to read. If you want to celebrate Hanukkah, or Christmas, or that new one," Mom said, looking at Karen for some help.

"Kwanza," Karen said.

"Right," Mom said. "Whatever you want to do, I'll try and help you out."

I was seven at the time and Karen was fourteen, but Karen was already reading about everything. I was more interested in pretending I was Luke Skywalker.

"Yea, though I walk through the valley of the shadow of death," the minister says. I know this one. I've heard it at every funeral I've ever been to. The old fraternity man sitting next to me stops his muttering and joins the minister in the recitation of the Twenty-third Psalm.

"Thy rod and thy staff, they comfort me," the Old Fraternity Guy says, then turns and looks at me. I'm staring at him. There are tears in his eyes. There are deep grooves in his face from years of smiling. He is a happy man, I think. A man not used to this sort of suffering. "Damn," he says, and for some reason I pat his hand like he is a child.

"There is no guilt greater than a life cut short," the minister says.

This I doubt.

After the service, Julie and I walk hand in hand down a steep, grassy hill where the burial will take place. My broken foot keeps buckling. It feels like someone is yanking my toes out one by one. Julie is chain-smoking.

"Lonnie," Julie says, giving my hand an extra squeeze, "I can't thank you enough for coming with me. This is all very difficult to fathom."

"I know," I say.

"But you've made some excellent contacts," she says.

"Invaluable," I say.

There is a depression cut into the grass and a mound of dirt covered by an AstroTurf tarp. The pallbearers, all beefy-looking executive types who have "probably played some ball," have already placed Bill Jennings's coffin onto the lowering platform.

When my grandfather died, I was only nine years old. I remember going to the funeral in my uncle Chad's cool convertible Cadillac with the top down. It was summer then, too, but we were in San Francisco. I remember holding my breath through the Caldecot tunnel and again coming over the Bay Bridge. Something back then made me always want to hold my breath. I used to tell Karen that I was just trying to prepare myself for the unlikely event of a water landing. But that wasn't it. I used to like that rush my body got when it had to breathe—when it had to finally wrestle control away from me before I did anything permanent.

I bite my lip and try it again. I stuff as much air as I can into my lungs and I say to myself, Okay, no more breathing until I say so. No more breathing until Bill Jennings is in the ground and they are throwing dirt on his casket.

Old Fraternity Guy is standing beside me muttering again.

I think I can hold my breath for at least two minutes. Maybe more.

"I appreciate what you did in there," Old Fraternity Guy says.

I nod my head.

"We were at SC together in the sixties," he says. "Pledged together. Drank a lot of brews, played a lot of football."

I'm starting to see spots.

"But, you know, people lose touch. I went to Vietnam and he went to the Coast Guard, that kind of shit," he says.

My ears are getting hot.

"Hadn't talked to him since eighty-two, but we were fraternity brothers," he says. "Whatever that means."

Here it comes. I can feel a cool burning in my chest. I fight it. I fight my lungs and my throat and my brain.

"I guess I always thought that I'd be in this place before Bill," he says.

I tighten my diaphragm. Old Fraternity Guy is a big black spot.

The minister starts reading a prayer. Bill Jennings's wife is crying very loudly. Bill Jennings's mother is bellowing. Julie is clutching my arm in a vise grip. Old Fraternity Guy puts a big paw on my shoulder and whispers into my ear.

"There just aren't many gentlemen left, is all I want to say, so I thank you."

My breath erupts from my lungs like a deep, mournful sob. A few people turn and look in my direction. Julie squeezes my arm and Old Fraternity Guy pats my hand.

Julie and I go out for drinks after the funeral. We drop off Julie's car at her house in Glendale and take the Mustang into Silverlake. It is near three o'clock when we finally take a seat in the back of a dive bar off Los Feliz.

"I like to come here," Julie says, lighting a cigarette despite the various no smoking signs littered on the walls. By the smell of the place, she's not the first person to blatantly break the health code. Julie waves her cigarette in the air when she talks. "It's very un-Hollywood. I can't stand that whole scene."

"Me either," I say.

Julie orders a martini, and with the memory of my stomach being pumped still very fresh in my mind, I order a glass of 7-Up. We sit in the dark booth for an hour talking about the things people generally talk about on a first date.

Julie gets up to go to the bathroom after her fourth martini, and when she comes back, she slides in beside me. I smell fresh perfume on her skin, something my mother used to wear. I notice that Julie has powdered her face.

The waitress comes back over, and, thinking what the hell, I say, "I'll have a shot of vodka." And I'm thinking: So this is how situations become situations. Avoid this one, Lonnie. Creep on out of your skin and don't make it worse. "And something for the lady."

"I can't get over Bill," Julie says. She is so close to me that I can smell the air that is coming out of her nose. "He had so much going for him."

Julie tilts her head down and lets it rest against my arm.

Here's my cue. "A terrible loss," I say.

Julie stares up at me, her eyes wide and red, and I know what is coming. I know because this is the real world and in the real world things happen exactly as they should. I don't have the advantage of a rising musical score to let me know if a sad scene is coming or if the monster is about to jump out of the closet. I just have wretched personal experience.

Julie touches my face with the back of her hand.

Now would be a good time to be a sufferer of chronic halitosis.

"You have beautiful skin," Julie says.

So you go through the motions of life for twenty-six years. You make decisions based on complete rational thought. You drive a sensible car because that's the kind of guy you are. You take a job that pays your bills and that's it. Punch in and out every day, shop at IKEA with the money you save, and buy your family Christmas gifts they appreciate.

"Do you want to kiss me?" Julie asks. Her lips touch mine when she speaks.

Maybe in college you "share" yourself with a few girls you meet at frat parties. There's that one that you get pregnant and sure, you joke with your friends about it for years afterward, but sometimes you wonder if that was your chance. You date women who wear bare midriffs. They sleep around on you, but that's okay because you are doing the same.

Julie is squeezing my thigh so hard that I can feel her nails in my skin. Her breath is stale and acrid and her tongue is revolving in concentric circles in my mouth.

So you fuck your boss in the backseat of your co-worker's tricked-out Mustang. You drive to your boss's pleasant house in Glendale, she blows you in the driveway, and then you have animal sex in every position imaginable. She calls out your name like it is a religious chant and all you are thinking is one thing: Claire.

I call the police from Charlie's that night.

"We have a fingerprint match from your apartment," a Detective Collins tells me. "Do you associate with any known felons?"

"No," I say. I've lied to so many people recently that lying to the police comes pretty easily.

"Our concern is for your safety, Mr. Milton," the detective says.

"I understand that," I say, "but that doesn't change anything."

Detective Collins clears his throat and I imagine he is a barrel-chested man wearing a tweed jacket. "Let me clue you in on something," he says. "What we're working on is a lot larger than someone stealing your couch and some of your clothes. I'm trying to quell an epidemic of theft."

Charlie walks into the living room and sees me lying face up on the *Star Wars* futon. I am still wearing Charlie's clothes, except the dress shirt he lent me doesn't have any buttons on it anymore. Julie likes it rough and frenzied. When he sees that his shirt is torn and that it is also covered in bright red lipstick, he turns around and walks back into his bedroom.

"I know I'm low on the crime totem pole," I say. "I just want my couch back." I give Detective Collins my work phone number and he tells me he will be in contact with me. I walk into Charlie's bedroom and all he can do is glare at me. He has the front page of the newspaper in his hand.

"I don't know what happened," I say.

"There are two things that separate men from women," Charlie says as though I haven't spoken. And to be honest, I don't know if I have. "Number one, men are wipe-and-go creatures. Doesn't matter if we're having sex or going to the bathroom. It's just boom-boom, wipe and go. No thinking about it or contemplating it. No guilt. You following me?"

"Yes," I say.

"Number two is this business of self-destruction," Charlie says. "We don't sit around beating ourselves. It's just jungle logic that moves us. One big rolling pheromone. None of this sappy Barbra Streisand crap."

Charlie takes three steps and is right in front of my face. I can see the zit hole he has picked into his chin. He smells like Irish Spring soap.

"You are in deep shit," Charlie says, unfolding the newspaper in front of my face. On the front page is a photo, albeit fuzzy, of Claire and me at Mistral. "And if I were you, I'd wipe and go."

Eleven

Two Vicodin later and I'm on the 405 heading toward Claire's. I'm in my Tercel because Charlie wants to wash the smell out of his Mustang before it gets a chance to set. Fog rolls over the mountains and makes the lights from the Getty Museum look dull and vacant. The Vicodin doesn't help.

My mind feels like boiling water. I can't keep one thought on the top before another one surfaces. No one would recognize me from the newspaper. I look like a smudge of newsprint eating some pasta with a beautiful woman. I mean, I know it's me, but who else would recognize that tuft of hair that sticks up toward the back of my scalp?

Fake. Liar. Cheat.

Things could definitely be worse. I could be in a Nazi prison camp eating my own skin under the guise of scientific examination.

Claire didn't call me today. No messages on the answering machine. No calls to Charlie's. Zero. Zilch.

I could be a sewer rat living off of other people's waste.

She said she would contact me on Sunday.

I could be Julie, asleep on the wet spot with my saliva drying on her breasts.

She probably got busy.

There was a message from my mother. She said it was hot in San Francisco and she couldn't wait to come to L.A. so that she could go to the beach.

Go bathe in the sun and let your body absorb the cancer.

I haven't slept in a very long time.

There was a message from the Staff Genius answering service telling me that two customer-service clerks were calling in sick for their temp jobs at Dynamic Solutions. I don't blame them. Dynamic Solutions makes and sells prosthetic arms. They have a huge mail order and Internet catalogue of fancy designer arms for every occasion.

I could be missing an arm. I could have a hook for a hand and a patch over an eye.

I exit the 405 on Wilshire and wind through Brentwood on San Vicente. There are people everywhere. A dozen coffee houses next door to a dozen bagel shops across the street from a dozen Kinko's. All of them are open twenty-four hours a day just in case you need them. Just in case you need to photocopy sensitive material while drinking a café mocha and eating a garlic bagel topped with creamy onion sauce and lox.

And these people sit and stare. They are doing culture. They aren't reading or even talking; they're just being beautiful. I wish I were beautiful. Or someone who believes he or she is.

Like Claire. Like if she sat down at this Starbucks or that Manhattan Bagel people would turn and look at her and think, Now she's got something going on.

What's wrong with wanting that?

I've just been killing time. So there's no difference between these Starbucks people and myself. I've never wanted my fifteen minutes to come when I wasn't paying attention.

I park my car behind a Wells Fargo bank and for a long time I just walk. My foot feels warm from the drugs and the air outside is still. I pass a newsstand and see myself eating dinner. I hand the attendant a quarter and he gives me the paper without hesitation. There is a missing girl in Palm Springs. Three hikers are believed dead in the Angeles forest. The President thinks we might be forced to bomb Iraq. And Claire and I are enjoying a pleasant meal.

The restaurant where O.J. Simpson's ex-wife left her sunglasses—and then forever changed TV—is closed and boarded up, but that doesn't stop a tourist couple from asking me to take a photo of them.

"Just point and click," the husband says.

I know Claire will be gone by the time I get to her house. I know that she will have seen the newspaper, will have seen her face halftoned and then reprinted a million times. She will have already climbed into her Saab, top down for effect, and have dashed off into the sunset. Dramatic music blaring from her stereo will follow her down the 405 or the 101, and the credits will roll right over my superimposed face as I am being hauled off to prison.

It's the Vicodin.

I walk through the neighborhood just surrounding Claire's. The houses are closer to the street here, so I can just make out the blue glow of television sets. Tom Brokaw is talking about the Fleecing of America. Dan Rather is selling the nation soybean futures without even knowing it. Maybe a maid is clearing away sorbet dishes and serving the chocolate soufflé.

Maybe someone is sitting on an expensive leather couch and staring back at me. Staring and saying to himself, "I know that guy. I saw him at a restaurant. Or the hospital. Or at old Bill's funeral. I saw him somewhere."

I pass a blue Cape Cod with the blinds drawn wide. In the front room several older couples are dancing the box step, or the swing, or something. I can't hear the music but I'm sure it's Artie Shaw or Glenn Miller.

I'm drowning in my skin. I am a block away from Claire's house, and I can't make my body move. My feet just won't turn the next corner. My hands won't pull themselves from my hair. Because I know she is gone. I stand and watch the couples dance for an hour at least. They move so gracefully. They stop and kiss sometimes. I just want to sit down in a field of sand and listen to their feet move on what I am sure is polished hardwood.

But instead I turn the corner. I turn and see the flashing lights of the police cars. The flashing lights of the ambulance that is screeching off down the street. The flashing lights of the Channel 4 news crew.

It doesn't hurt me to say it can't be love. If you can't talk about it, it isn't love. If you can't cross the police lines to find out who is dead, or who is shot, or who is anything, then you aren't in love. If this is love, then we need to consider the ramifications. Fight the Battle of the Bulge or storm the beach at Normandy and just get right down to the answers. She is not Cleopatra. Age *can* wither her and custom *can* stale her infinite variety, I would tell Mark Antony.

But this is real.

I stay awake all night telling Charlie everything.

Twelve

"Let me get one thing straight," Charlie says. We're in the Staff Genius bathroom. It's nine in the morning on Monday. "You never paid for a damn thing?"

"The cab," I say. "I always paid for the cab."

Charlie zips up and checks his face in the mirror. "Well," he says, "it's not like you killed someone, right?"

I didn't tell him about Bill Jennings. Not even Charlie is that understanding. "Right," I say. "But I don't know who was in that ambulance."

"Worst-case scenario," Charlie says, "it was some kid pissing on the hedges and the owner of the house capped him. People in that area are sensitive about their grounds."

"Then what's the best?"

"Your little *femme fatale* choked on some stolen filet mignon and you're golden. You walk into the police station and say that crazy chick made you do some fucked-up things and now you are throwing yourself on the mercy of the court. A little freeway cleanup, some restitution, and you're walking without a scratch on you."

"I don't think it's that simple anymore," I say. "This isn't some movie. There are consequences."

"This is L.A.," Charlie says. "Tell the police you've got an agent and you want to negotiate some kind of settlement. You think the cops aren't thinking back-end numbers on every arrest?"

When I get back to my desk, there is a sealed envelope on my chair. I pick it up and smell the powdery perfume that Julie wears. The envelope is cream colored and soft. There is a faint red rose printed on the back.

I look up and Julie smiles at me from the door to her office. She is wearing a low-cut sweater that highlights her sagging breasts. She turns her head and points to a noticeable bite mark on her neck. There's another at the base of her throat.

You diseased fuck, I think. As soon as Julie walks back into her office, I pull out the bottle of Vicodin I have in my pocket and dump its remains into the paper shredder. I don't care if my foot turns the color of a dog's gums. I can live with the pain.

Mondays are the worst days at Staff Genius. Every person who got fired on Friday shows up in his or her most expensive outfit right when the doors open. They sit in the lobby and smile, chat up the receptionist, and tell lies about why their last job wasn't "a good fit." They've never been fired. They've been downsized. There was a personality clash with a co-worker. New software was installed that meant a decrease in "as needed" clerical staff. It was simply time for a change.

I sit at my desk and stare at them. There are three women, two men, and a woman who is obviously a man in drag. They copy their résumés word for word onto our exclusive Staff Genius Employment Questionnaire. They drink our exclusive Staff Genius Coffee (supplied by Corporate, by way of Yuban), eat our exclusive Staff Genius Doughnuts, and sweat on our exclusive Staff Genius faux leather couches, all while waiting for the crucial interview to be conducted by one of Staff Genius's elite crew of Staffing Professionals.

And here I am with my broken foot stuffed into a thick black sock, my last Vicodin pureed into a fine dust by the shredder, and my boss is giving me the come-fuck-me eye.

Charlie stops in front of my desk. He's holding the Metro section of the *Times* in his hands. "Not a scenario I imagined," he says and drops the paper onto my desk. There is a full-color photo of a man in a body bag. The headline says:

MILLIONAIRE SLAIN NEAR BRENTWOOD ESTATE

I buzz the receptionist. "Send me an applicant," I say. "In fact, send me all the applicants. I want to interview every single person who walks through the door today."

There are a lot of things I don't know. I don't know why we've never annexed Canada. I don't know why we let a man as old as Dick Clark sit in the freezing cold every New Year's Eve just to tell us the time. And, mostly, I don't know why I haven't stuck a gun in my mouth.

Julie calls me into her office as I'm leaving for lunch. "Not trying to escape, I hope," she says.

"I've got a doctor's appointment," I say. "Foot's bothering me."

"Didn't seem to bother you yesterday," Julie says. "Did you read my note?"

"Not yet," I say. "I wanted to do it in private."

"It's private in here."

"Right," I say.

Julie walks around to the front of her desk. "It wasn't very polite of you just to leave me there wanting more."

"Right."

"Do you want to meet after work?"

"My mom is in town," I say. And then I remember: My mom *is* in town. "We're going to dinner."

"I guess it's too early for me to meet the family," Julie says.

I want to tell Julie that she's a nice woman. I want to tell her that we've made a mistake. I was under the influence of painkillers; enough painkillers, in fact, to really cloud my better judgment. I want to say, Water under the bridge. No hard feelings, right? Can't ruin the sanctity of the office dynamics. Especially since I consider you a mentor.

"Right," I say.

I sit in Jerry's Deli and stare at the words in the newspaper. They don't move. They don't jump off of the page and strangle me. They simply sit there and snicker. They say, Lonnie, you've made a big mistake. In fact, Mr. Milton, aside from fucking your boss (which was pretty epic if we do say so ourselves), and of course completely disregarding the fact that you've personally been responsible for a brand-new wave of crime in this fair city, we think the police might like to talk to you as soon as they finish collecting the forensic evidence at the scene of a pretty gruesome crime. So, go ahead and order yourself a great big corned beef sandwich. Shoot, get some mayo on it and have that nice waitress cut you a slice of German chocolate cake. Because you know what? You know what, BIG FELLA? You are going to jail.

> BRENTWOOD—In a scene reminiscent of another crime of passion, millionaire financier Pejman Barlavi was found stabbed last night in front of his Brentwood estate. Barlavi, 37, was discovered by two joggers in front of his wooded compound. He had been stabbed several times in both the neck and chest and died from apparent blood loss. Sources indicated that the police were processing evidence found at the scene, including the suspected murder weapon, an ivory-handled knife . . .

Go ahead and call your sister and tell her you can't wait for the big family dinner tonight because, boy, you just love everyone. Call Karen and tell her where it is you want your last supper because as soon as the police process those fingerprints, and let's not forget the videotape, they'll see you. They'll see you standing in the shadows as they wheel off poor Mr. Barlavi. And your fingerprints! You just had to touch everything, didn't you? Had to have a bagel that morning, didn't you? Had to twist that knife in your hand because you couldn't believe someone was wealthy enough to cut his bagels using such an expensive knife.

I fold the newspaper in half, and in half again, and again until the color photo of Pejman Barlavi is just a single black line. Until all those words have shut their cake holes.

A waitress stands in front of my table and stares at me. She's smiling—her perfect little rows of white teeth clamped together so tightly that it hurts me to look at her.

"We've got a bet," she says, pointing over her shoulder at two other waitresses. "And I've been commissioned to find out the truth."

I don't say anything for a long time. She has teased blond hair and overdone eye makeup. If she were smart, I think, she'd be walking up and down Sunset instead of serving lunch.

"What do you win?" I ask.

She glances over her shoulder. Her friends giggle and hold on to each other. "Nothing," she says, turning back around. "Self-fulfillment, maybe?"

Zen and the Art of Sandwich Delivery.

"I'm not sure who you are," she says, her cheeks reddening, "but I'm sure you're somebody. Am I right?"

Before I can answer her, before I can open up the cover of the Metro section of the *L.A. Times* to prove to her that maybe she doesn't want to ask that question, I see a man and a woman sit down at the table across from me. He's wearing a tuxedo. She's wearing a black, flowing evening gown and a diamond necklace. It is one-fifteen on a Monday afternoon. It is the dead of summer. The Oscars aren't for another eight months, at least.

"I'm nobody," I say. "I'm just a guy trying to eat some lunch."

The waitress leans forward, hands on her hips. "That's cool," she says. "I think actors are just like normal people. You've just got a better job, right? I understand you not wanting to get noticed."

I nod to her. She nods to me. We nod to each other.

A lot of people come to Jerry's Deli for lunch. No one wears a tux.

The waitress shakes my hand and tells me she appreciates my desire for privacy, but I'm watching the well-dressed couple.

"You look like Garbo in that dress," he says.

"We'll be late for the premiere," she says.

They look around to see if anyone is watching them. He looks right at me and tries to pretend he doesn't see me. It's impossible. I'm shooting Vulcan death rays out of my eyes at him.

"What are you going to order, darling?" he says.

"Whatever the chef makes special," she says.

The demo goes for ten minutes. She orders the chicken fried steak (price: $11.95); he orders the short ribs (price: $13.99). They ask the waitress to bring them a bottle of Jerry's finest wine (Mondavi merlot 1995: $36.00).

I look at her necklace and decide that those "diamonds" are probably courtesy of QVC. His shoes are rentals. If he could afford to wear a tuxedo in the middle of the afternoon, then he could certainly afford classier shoes. There is a slight run along the back of her nylons. Not a big, screaming run, or even one of those divot runs. This one has been corrected. I see a little dab of nail polish at the base of it.

She catches me staring at her legs. I look up and she is regarding me with something less than scorn. She likes it. She likes it more than she likes worrying about breast cancer or about if she has enough cash in her account to cover all of her bills.

The first rule that Claire and I ever had was that we didn't use our own names. We never said anything that anyone could ever use against us. Claire would sit there and fuck every waiter in the place with her eyes. She would make every busboy want to lie about what he'd seen just by biting her lip.

"Finally," he whispers to her, "we're doing this!"

"Go home," I say and he turns and looks at me.

"Are you talking to me?"

"Nice day," I say to her. "Must be hot in those nylons."

"Do we know you?" he says. She starts tapping her fingers on a plate of bagel chips.

The waitress brings them their food and their $36 bottle of wine.

"Big awards ceremony at the Shrine tonight?" I say. "Maybe a fund-raiser to save the redwoods? Or something at the Getty? Is that it? Some kind of high-powered art house explosion on top of the hill?"

He starts to open his mouth, but she puts a hand up to stop him. "What do you want?" she says. "Is there something I can help you with?"

"Maybe," I say, "you can take those Home Shopping diamonds off your neck and cash them in to get some decent shoes for 007 over here."

Jerry's is packed. There is a line of people waiting to be seated. I see someone who looks a bit like the child star who became the adult drug addict. Not an A list crowd, for sure.

"We don't want any trouble," he says.

Two cops sit down at the counter.

I think about my apartment, about my IKEA couches and my Zenith TV. I think about the way I used to come home from work and watch videos on my Zenith TV while lying on my IKEA couches. I think about the day Staff Genius hired me and I told myself that it wouldn't be permanent. I'd get married, have some kids, buy myself an expensive watch, become more or less Bill Jennings, and then retire to a home in the Florida Keys.

007 balls up his napkin. Princess Diana of QVC toys with the clasp on her necklace.

Most people don't like the idea of having to fight. They think that they'll lose some of their teeth or someone will kick them in the groin or pull their hair. Nobody wants to collect their teeth or hair off the pavement.

"Enjoy your lunch," I say and drop a twenty onto my table, more than enough to cover my bill.

■ ■ ■

I can imagine what a man thinks when he sees a picture of a woman like Claire in the newspaper with a guy like me. He thinks, I could have a woman like that. If only I dressed or held myself better. They all think they can have her. They all think they're winning when they're just losing. Put on a tuxedo and grab some cheap imitation of Claire. Walk into a second-tier chain restaurant like Jerry's or California Pizza Kitchen and pretend you are the Bonnie and Clyde of petty crime.

I can picture every move these men make. They creep around corners. They wear suits that press against their skin like paste because they sweat. They sweat the details. They pay attention. They don't know how to play the role.

They do all the things they won't confess to the next day in church. Because men like 007 in Jerry's go to church on Sundays and apologize for all the things they've done Monday through Saturday. Like any of us can be saved.

Like when I walk out of Jerry's and see the row of TVs across the street at Circuit City all tuned to CNN. An entire picture window of Bernard Shaw. All I can see are Bernie's narrow lips and tight, angular eyes stuffed behind those glasses. Those glasses that say, "I'm smarter than you, so listen to the news I'm about to tell you."

There are two people standing in front of the picture window watching Bernie.

"It's terrible," a man in a long leather jacket says. He looks like Serpico.

"The way people just waste themselves," a woman in dark sunglasses says.

"All for food? Is it just for the food?" Serpico says.

There is no sound outside, but I know what I'm about to see. Bernie's face disappears, replaced by a live shot of an International House of Pancakes. Police stand five deep in the parking lot, guns drawn. The camera pans to a well-dressed couple standing near the front door. He is wearing a black suit. She is wearing a dress that makes her look like a mermaid.

"You know," Serpico says, turning to me, "it's this kind of thing that makes all of our insurance go up."

"You own a restaurant?"

"It doesn't matter what kind of business you're in, you know?" he says. "All comes out of the same pot."

The screen switches back to Bernard Shaw for a moment, his eyes dark and serious behind those glasses. He's staring right at me. He looks down and touches his left ear. I make out the words he mouths. He says, "This just in," or something close to it.

A limo is blocked by two police cars at the drive-through window of a Taco Bell. Cops with drawn weapons are everywhere.

They are all fakes. Droids. Dime-store paperbacks of the original.

"It's this whole X generation," the woman says.

"It's the millennium," Serpico says.

It's me. It's Claire. Everyone's got his own way to get hooked.

I've got to find Claire.

84

When I get back to Staff Genius, the receptionist hands me a thick stack of messages. One is from my mother, two are from Karen, three are from Maws and Company (the company that rents—or rented—my apartment), and two are from the LAPD.

The ones from the LAPD are marked "Urgent." I don't think they have found my couches.

"Who's Karen?"

I look up and Julie is standing in the lobby, a cigarette dangling from her lips. There is a dollop of dried mustard on her chin.

"Why?"

"She called for you," Julie says, pointing her cigarette at my handful of messages. "Twice."

"So did the police," I say. "So maybe you shouldn't go around looking at every scrap of paper with my name on it. It might save you some stress."

An Asian woman taking a typing test glares at me. I've interrupted her flow.

"You can't talk to me like that," Julie says. The folds in her neck start to redden. She looks like an angry turnip.

My grandfather once told me never to have an argument unless I could come out looking like a champion. Don't ever shout. Whisper if you can, make them hear you.

He told me to breathe when I talked. He told me to make every word sound important by inhaling and exhaling deeply between each point.

Claire told me to consider the conditions before I spoke. To make sure no one overheard anything important.

"She's my sister," I shout. "I'm fucking my sister!"

After Julie ran out of the office crying and after the Asian woman taking the typing test told me I was going to rot in hell for eternity, Charlie walked up and shook my hand.

"That's how you end a relationship gracefully," he said.

I apologize to Julie before I return any of my calls. I tell her that I'm under an awful amount of pressure. I tell her that with my broken foot, and my apartment, and with, you know, the *horror* of Bill Jennings, that I've just not been myself.

She touches my face. I want her hand to feel like rotted flesh. It doesn't.

"I know," she says. "I just get jealous."

I stare at the folds along her belly. I remember the way she just wouldn't stop fucking me. I think, Okay, tell her you meant everything you said earlier. Tell her that *this* excuse was just an excuse. You really are doing your sister and your sister is actually quite jealous, too.

"I understand," I say.

When I get back to my desk, there is a message from ADP, our payroll service, resting on my phone. It says they are having a problem processing the paycheck for Claire Gooden and that I am to call them immediately.

It takes a minute because the Vicodin dust has clogged the blades, but eventually the message from ADP is shredded into a hundred pieces.

■ ■ ■

"Mom wants to go to Mistral," Karen says. It is four-thirty. We've been playing phone tag. There is a fifty-five-year-old man sitting at my desk retaking a filing test. He can't figure out if The Smith Company comes before or after Thespian Theaters. He's been working as an accounts payable clerk for eleven years. He was recently downsized.

"She saw something in the newspaper about it," Karen says. "She thinks she'll see Tom Selleck there."

The man at my desk rips the test in half. "This is bullshit," he says. "I'm a professional."

"This isn't the DMV," I say, handing the man another test. "You don't leave until you pass."

"Are you talking to me?" Karen asks.

"No," I say. "I have someone at my desk."

"You know," Karen says, "I'm still pissed at you for the other night."

"I think Mistral is a bad choice," I say.

"Are you listening to me?" Karen says.

"No," I say, because I'm not. I'm glaring at the fifty-five-year-old downsized man who's sitting at my desk popping antacids to take a filing test. I'm staring at the way his forehead is sweating. I'm staring at his bloodshot little eyes that are so used to crunching numbers all day. Accounts payable for eleven years. For eleven years he wrote checks. He played around on the computer. First he had that DOS version of Lotus, then maybe QuarkXPress, then he moved up to Quicken and Quick Books, and then he was a pro on Excel, and then he probably got fired for being too old or too expensive.

"Are you still involved with that girl?" Karen asks.

"Yes," I say. Yes, because I'm about ten minutes away from a nervous breakdown.

"Is she coming tonight?"

"No," I say. "But she might be there."

"You're not making any sense to me," Karen says. "Are you still snorting Vicodin?"

"I poured them all into my paper shredder," I say.

"Good start," she says.

"We can't go to Mistral," I say.

"We'll meet you there at eight," Karen says and hangs up.

Mr. Downsized balls up the filing test and throws it on the floor. "You can't keep me here," he says.

"You're right," I say. "So why don't you go walk out the door and tell your beautiful wife and child that you can't work because you don't know how to file."

Mr. Downsized opens his mouth but doesn't say anything.

"Next week at this time," I say, "you and your pitiful family will be lucky to have a room at some dirtbag hotel downtown. Your wife will probably be sucking off some junkie and you'll be pacing the hallway waiting for the twenty bucks."

Charlie comes up behind me. "Lonnie," he says.

"Here's a clue," I say, pulling out another filing test. "*The* doesn't count!"

"Lonnie," Charlie says, and I turn around.

"What?" I shout. "What?"

Charlie looks scared. Mr. Downsized looks busy because he's taking that test with vigor usually reserved for paying accounts.

"Is this a problem I can help you with?" Charlie asks.

"No," I say. "I'm fine."

I look at my paper shredder and decide that if I had to, I could lick the Vicodin dust off the blades.

"I'm great," I say.

Julie sends me home ten minutes later after she overhears me telling Mr. Downsized that he might want to consider a career as a postal worker. I don't tell her that I don't really have a home anymore.

I try to check my messages from Charlie's. A recording comes on and tells me that my number, as of five P.M., is no longer in service. I call GTE and a wonderful service associate informs me that I am fourteen days late on my bill, again, and that my service has been canceled. She also tells me that the phone company is now offering cell phone service at just a fraction of the price both LA Cellular and Airtouch charge.

I call Maws and Company and they inform me that the locks on what was my apartment have been changed and that they are holding my possessions until my rent is paid up through the day they officially evicted me. They also tell me that they have obtained a restraining order against me and that if I step foot on the property they will use deadly force, if need be, to protect their employee Glen, who, they say, I tried to murder.

"After I pay my rent," I say, "how am I supposed to get my stuff back?"

"That really isn't my problem," says Yvette, my "case manager" at Maws and Company.

"Do you see the hypocrisy here, Yvette?" I ask. "I mean, just as a person, not as my case manager."

"Mr. Milton," she says, "I really don't care."

I pick up the phone to call the LAPD and then decide better of it. If they wanted to talk to me, they could have shown up at my office. It's not as if they don't know where I work.

Or where I eat.

It's seven o'clock and I need to meet my mother and sister in an hour at a place I have recently robbed. A place that probably has a picture of the cowlick on the back of my head blown up and framed.

And I have nothing to wear.

I troll through Charlie's closet and find a pair of black rayon slacks and a sweater vest. I cover my foot with a black sock. They won't be looking for a guy wearing a soft cast covered by a black sock.

I slick my hair back with Charlie's gel and splash some cologne on my face that smells like a mixture of chocolate mint ice cream and a eucalyptus tree. I'm sure Charlie would tell me both are natural aphrodisiacs.

The mirror tells me I look like a star. It tells me I'm untouchable. It says, Jake, that's right, *Jake,* this is your world, baby, the rest of us are just taking up space.

I'm invisible.

I'm a shadow.

Like the song says, I think. I am Superman.

Thirteen

I'm screwed.

Half a mile from Mistral I see the flashing lights. There are at least ten police cars parked on Ventura Boulevard. Cops are stationed in front of Mistral and its next-door neighbor La Fondue Bourguignonne. They're shining flashlights into cars. People are being questioned on the street and here I am looking like I walked out of central casting. Yes, Officer, I'm here for the role of felon. Is that part filled yet?

I pull off Ventura and head north on Woodman. I have a simple solution to a difficult problem. There's a Marshalls on the corner of Woodman and Riverside. I go inside and buy a pair of defective Calvin Klein khakis for the low-low-priced-to-move-only-at-Marshalls amount of nine dollars. The only defect I can find is that the right pant leg is slightly longer than the left. No problem here.

I find a blue-and-yellow-striped Ralph Lauren polo shirt for fourteen dollars. The collar buttons funny. It makes my neck look pinched. It's perfect.

In the mirror, I look like me. I look like you. I look like anybody.

■ ■ ■

There's a black Porsche clogging the valet lane in front of Mistral. I nudge my Tercel in behind it and step out. A police officer is sitting in the front seat of the Porsche shining a penlight into every crevice he can find. Another officer has a man in handcuffs who looks like Tony Curtis.

The valet walks up to my car and I hand him my keys.

"Do you have a reservation?" he asks, looking at my car.

"Yes," I say.

"Are you sure?"

A red limo pulls in front of the Porsche and Drew Barrymore steps out.

"Yeah," I say, "I'm here with Drew."

The valet hands me a ticket. "You'll need to show this to the officer at the door," he says. "In case they want to look at your car, which I doubt."

I wait in line while Drew and her party are ushered inside. The police obviously know that Drew Barrymore and her friends would never be involved in the heisting of food. They probably eat for free anyway.

When I get to the door, the police officer puts a hand up to stop me. "Hold on there, Buck," he says. "You got a reservation?"

"Do you work for the restaurant?" I ask.

The officer glares at me. He's wearing a Kevlar vest over his uniform and has a handgun strapped over his shoulder. Judging by the bulge on his ankle, he has another, smaller gun stored there.

"Simple question, Buck," he says. "No need to get smart. Lotta people with frayed nerves standing around out here and I personally don't need your lip. So yes or no?"

"Yes," I say. "I'm meeting my mother here."

A smirk cracks around the cop's mouth, as if he has a hundred good lines he could say, but all of them would get him in trouble in this new ultra PC environment.

"Lemme see your ticket," he says finally and I hand it to him. "In order to enter the restaurant you must agree to the following conditions, you following me so far?"

"Sure," I say and then I see the front page of Sunday's *Times* blown up and placed on a sandwich board behind the cop. My cowlick is a foot high. There is no sauce on my pasta. Claire's head is the size of a small child.

"Number one," the cop says, reading from a three-by-five-inch card. "You agree to allow officers of the LAPD to search your automobile pending any probable cause as outlined by both Mistral and the United States Constitution. Number two, you agree that you will pay for your meal or face criminal prosecution. And three, you waive all rights to sue Mistral or any of its affiliated companies without arbitration."

"I do," I say. "I waive everything."

The cop moves to one side and lets me pass.

"Enjoy your meal," he says, but he means, "Fuckin' mama's boy."

All of which is fine. He never even looked at the sandwich board.

I find my mom and my sister sitting at a table by the window.

"Did you see Drew Barrymore?" Mom asks after she hugs me. "She's sitting at the bar just like a normal person."

"She is a normal person," I say.

"You know her?" Mom asks.

"Lonnie knows everyone," Karen says. She's tried to cover the hickey on her neck with makeup, but it's still noticeable.

"What'd you do to your foot?" Mom asks.

"I was kicking all the single women away from my door," I say. Mom reaches across the table and pinches my cheek.

"You never lose that charm, do you?" she says. "I called your apartment and they said your number was out of service. Too many girls calling?"

"Something like that," I say.

Karen passes me a bottle of merlot. "Mom's treating," she says, and I think she's offering a kind of mutual truce. "Drink up."

I pour myself a glass and look around the restaurant. Every table is filled and the bar is overflowing. Nothing attracts a crowd like a crowd.

I see our waiter before I am even able to process the information. He's smiling. He's tall and handsome. He's waving.

I'm caught.

"Hey," he says, extending his hand toward mine, "remember me?"

I stare at his chiseled features and a sense of real dread runs over me. "You worked somewhere else, didn't you?"

"Yeah," he says. "Remember, you tried to get me a job? I worked at Intermezzo."

"Oh," I say. "Right. Rick, isn't it?"

Rick Kite, I think. I owe you money. I owe you a big dinner with a gracious tip and then I need to get the hell out of here.

"Yeah," he says, "you got it."

We tell Rick that we still need a few more minutes and he says, "No problem," and pats me on the back like we are old pals.

"Is that why you didn't want to come here?" Karen asks. "Couldn't get that guy a job?"

"Right," I say. "Very embarrassing."

"How is your job?" Mom asks.

"I'm staffing the world," I say. "In a couple weeks I open up the office in Encino." I'm in charge in three weeks. Three weeks until I become Julie. Three weeks until I become middle management. "It's going to be a real challenge."

"Just take it one receptionist at a time," Karen says, pouring another glass of wine.

A news crew is setting up for a remote broadcast outside on the street. Mom taps on the window with one of her long, natural, never-Lee-Press-On-nails. "You see that?" she says. "That's smart reporting. Setting up at the scene of the crime in case the perp shows up again."

"Perp?" I say.

Mom ignores me, fascinated by the Action News van. "Did you know the first wire-to-wire live telecast of breaking news was done in 1949?"

"I had no idea," I say. Karen isn't paying attention. She just keeps pouring herself more wine.

"It's true," she says. "A little girl fell down a well and they covered her rescue for twenty-seven straight hours. It was amazing. I remember your grandfather dragged us to a Fleenor's Market that had a TV and we watched for hours while they tried to get that poor child out."

"And now look," I say. "You could be watching history from the comfort of a fine restaurant."

"That girl died," Mom says. "I remember when they pulled her limp body out. I was just a kid, but it's as clear to me today as any of those awful high-speed chases are. And it meant something, you know what I mean, Karen?"

Karen's not listening. She's staring at a table of young men. They are all wearing sunglasses. "Sorry," Karen says after I nudge her with my foot. "Wasn't paying attention. I think one of those guys is somebody."

"Just someone with a better job than us," I say.

Rick comes back to our table and I order the filet mignon. Karen and Mom both order seafood. "Really good to see you," I say to Rick before he leaves with our order. "Glad you landed on your feet."

"I'm just hoping the couple that stiffed me comes back in here," he says.

"Back?"

"Yeah," he says. "That's their picture up front. I recognized the girl immediately, and I couldn't forget the way that guy had that stupid hair sticking straight up off the back of his head."

"Hard to miss," I say.

"I think this whole dinner theft thing is terrible," Mom says after Rick has left. "There's just no respect for commerce anymore. People can't wait to rip someone off."

"I don't agree with that," I say. "Maybe these people are just trying to sample the good life."

"Get a better job," Karen says, still staring at the table of men. "Then you can eat at these places all the time."

"I saw on the news today that it's really becoming an epidemic," Mom says. "That couple in the paper are real urban legends. I'm surprised they don't have their own cult by now."

A line of people waits outside to get in Mistral. There are men in expensive Italian suits, women in designer gowns. The waiters inside are buzzing. There is money in that line. They can taste it, I'm sure. What they probably don't see are the tourists in their Planet Hollywood souvenir wear looking for the real Planet Hollywood.

We sit in Mistral, eat our dinner, and make small talk.

There are skeletons in this restaurant and I see them everywhere. I watch Mom and Karen eat and I wonder if they think I am acting strange. Do they notice when I bow my head when a familiar face walks by the table? Do they see that I am looking at every woman who walks through the door, even though I know Claire would never come back?

Would she?

Might she walk through this door just because she can? Because she thinks she is as invisible as I am. Except that there is a dead man. Except that all this dying started with her. Here I am sitting at Mistral with Mom and Karen and all they can talk about is TV and *Dateline NBC* and that strange couple in the newspaper who robbed this very restaurant and what if they are sitting at the same table as those two. Talk about bad karma, they are saying.

I fill in the blanks of their conversation. I bring up topics and I pretend to listen and then I wonder if all this dying started because I was a little tired of my life and Claire was intimate with hers. Made me feel wanted.

Karen starts talking about past-life regression and about the support group she joined for children whose fathers were deadbeats and how I should sign up. She says it would make me less distant and cold and less likely to get tangled up with women who make me break my feet. I think our truce is over, but I still don't want to fight.

In group, Karen is saying, emotions are the norm. She says I might be able to really connect with my inner self and answer some tough personal questions. I tell Karen that it all sounds terrific, but what I'm thinking is that all of these people outside in line are here because they read the paper. Because they are the people who obsess about the lives of a population they will never know. They sit in their living rooms and watch *Entertainment Tonight* until they think they really understand Brad Pitt.

They form relationships with pictures.

"Some restorative physical contact would be good for you," Karen says to me.

Mom nods her head. "It's true," she says. "Oprah was just saying the same thing."

Yes, I tell them, all of this sounds great. I am aware that my mother and sister are currently doing some kind of intervention on me, so I pretend to really listen to what they are saying. Karen's offering of wine to me earlier was no cease-fire, I've figured out, but a way to get me talking and relaxed. Mom is now digging in on me.

"I've heard all about this Claire girl," she says, and I think she really has. Mom is just like the street people. Her knowledge is gleaned from whatever Stone Phillips has to say on *Dateline* and is reinforced by whatever she reads in the paper the next morning.

Mom tells me about myself. She informs me that I have always cried out for role models ever since Dad left, that I'm in desperate need of a woman who can straighten me out, stop me from fucking up (and I now know she is serious because she says "fuck"), and right my ship.

I'm agreeing to everything.

I'll pick someone special.

I've kind of been seeing my boss, who's, well, *mature*.

I've been telling my friend Charlie how I really feel.

Claire is just another girl.

I just want someone who wants to walk on the beach.

Go to IKEA.

Extort some money from high-ranking health-care officials and then make them plummet to their deaths.

"That's not funny," Mom says. "I saw that man on TV."

"I think you'll really love meditating," Karen says.

I pull down my menu of positive responses. I look at my mother and sister and think I should just stop lying, turn myself in to the police, tell them all I can about Claire and about that man Pac-Man or whatever the hell his name was who bled to death from stab wounds.

"This has really helped," I say.

Mom reaches across the table and takes my hand. "Lonnie," she says, "we just don't want you to end up like one of those people we see on TV. It's just not worth it."

We walk out of Mistral just in time to see the news the Action News crew has been expecting. Facedown on the pavement in front of La Fondue Bourguignonne is a man in a gorgeous black suit and a woman in a skintight red dress.

"My God," Mom says. "Is that them?"

A police helicopter swoops across Ventura Boulevard showering the street with light. The crowd of people waiting to get into Mistral are snapping pictures and rolling their video cameras.

"I think that's a Bob Mackie dress," a woman standing next to my mother says. "And that suit is definitely Armani."

Two police officers draped in Kevlar stand over the couple and all I can think is that none of these people know what they are doing. You don't just show up in an Armani suit and think you can eat for free. There's a method.

Armani-man lifts up his head and I think he's about to say something. I think he's going to make an impassioned plea for an end to animal testing. I think he's going to whip out a handmade sign that says "Fuck the HMOs" or "No More Assisted Suicide." Instead, he lifts up his head and says four little words that should mean just about nothing to all of us good people out enjoying a fine meal:

"This is for Lonnie!"

Problem Number One: It means something to me.

Problem Number Two: When Armani-man finished shouting, he reached inside his jacket and the cop standing above him fired four shots into the back of his skull.

Problem Number Three: Action News coming to you live from the San Fernando Valley where terror has erupted in front of two posh dining spots . . .

He said my name.

He didn't say Jake. He didn't say Claire. He said Lonnie.

"Let's go," I say to my mom and sister. "You can watch this on TV when you get home."

"Did he say 'This is for Lonnie'?" Karen asks. "Did he really say that?"

There are flashing lights coming from every direction. There is an ambulance. I see a fire truck. Eyewitness News pulls up in their sleek Metro News van, blue siren lights spinning on top, just like in the commercials. The Channel 5 Urgent News chopper swings over the top of Mistral like an Apache fighter helicopter and hovers above the crowd. It looks like it wants to open fire.

"No," I say.

"He did," Mom says.

The girl in the tight red dress is covered in blood. She's lying there on Ventura Boulevard in a five-thousand-dollar dress with her friend's brains rolling toward her. There's a paramedic pounding on Armani-man's chest and he's screaming, "Breathe!" but it's useless because Armani-man doesn't have a head anymore.

"For a woman," Karen says. "All this for a woman?"

The girl in the tight red dress is sitting up now, sobbing. She's young, maybe eighteen, and her makeup is smeared across her face. There's lipstick on her nose. Eyeliner runs down her cheeks in thick black streaks. She doesn't even notice the blood in her hair or on her left ear. It's probably her mother's dress. Maybe tonight is a sorority formal. Maybe she and Armani-man met at an Orange Julius last fall and have been dating ever since.

"It was never just about a woman," I say.

"That little girl who fell in the well," Mom says. "That's what started all of this."

"I can't believe that guy would get his brains blown out just for a woman," Karen says. "May I never have that power over someone."

You're a brave man, I say to myself. You're in control of your own destiny. You get people jobs, I say. Do you have any idea how much good karma that equals out to? Every time you get some guy a job doing data entry for six bucks an hour, you're getting another big star. Every time someone gets hired for a permanent job and then gets a raise, a 401(K), and two weeks' paid vacation, man, check the mirror and look for your halo.

He said my name.

No matter how many times a legal secretary buys me a dozen Mrs. Fields cookies for getting her a job with an environmental law firm, nothing is going to replace the fact that there's a guy wearing his cerebellum on Ventura Boulevard.

I need to sit down and write myself a long letter. I need to tell myself that all of these things going on aren't really happening. It's like watching *The Real World* on MTV. Those people are real, they live and they breathe, but nothing that happens to them actually happens in real life. No one ever moves into a posh spread in New York or Los Angeles or even Seattle and then gets to have deep, meaningful conversations with their seven carefully selected sexually ambiguous roommates. No one lives rent-free in a major American city unless they live on the street.

No one witnesses a man getting blown away after shouting his or her name. It just doesn't happen.

I'm a dreamer, I know that's my problem. My mom told me at dinner that I could never tell when I wasn't being realistic.

I stare at the girl in the tight red dress. I see her curves and her hair and I think I can almost smell her perfume. She's not Claire, for sure, but she has something that makes me want to tell her that she will understand all of this eventually. This is all black and white, I would tell her. One day you'll own an Aerostar and everything will be fine.

The paramedics lift Armani-man onto a stretcher. The cops pick up his clothes from the pavement and rifle through the pockets. They pull out a copy of yesterday's *L.A. Times* front page.

I don't have to understand all of this to know it's not all right. Sometime tonight, maybe while I was enjoying my filet mignon, these two kids heard my name on the news. Heard that the person on the front page of the *L.A. Times* was named Lonnie Milton and he was wanted for questioning.

Wanted for murder? Maybe.

"What happened to the days when people were discovered at soda fountains?" Mom says. "When did that stop?"

"Let's get out of here," Karen says, slipping one arm through mine and another through Mom's. "Before one of us gets shot."

I get in my car and drive up the 101 and then over Topanga until I reach Malibu. I park my Tercel on PCH and stare at the lights from the

Santa Monica Pier flickering against the sky. In another time or place, for any other person, this would be a place to look out and think romantic thoughts. I can envision bringing a woman here to propose marriage. I can picture us taking a moonlit walk across the beach, and then I'd stop and drop to one knee. I would say all the right words and I'd make all the right moves with my hands. I would touch her face gently and tell her that I would keep her like a monument. I would polish our love and shine it until it was the only thing we could ever see, ever think, ever want.

I get out of the car and stand on the shoulder watching the Ferris wheel make its slow revolutions. A desperate man never knows much about love, I think. And maybe that's why I'm here alone.

I watch the lights glitter for a long while, until time feels like a disease, until I know that if I go home, if I had a home, that I could turn on the TV and see my face on the news. And there would be my name and somewhere my mother would be dialing my phone number and getting that same recording I got, and Karen would call Charlie's and he would say he hadn't seen me since I told Mr. Downsized that he should be a postal carrier.

There's an extraordinary wall of sound popping in my head and I figure it must be the Vicodin wearing off. It's the shock of seeing Armani-man blown away as an after-dinner treat. It's one more night without Claire, whom I'm starting to think rationally about.

I think that this is all her. All the dead people are Claire. And I know, for the first time, that nobody is Claire. Especially not Claire.

Fourteen

It's past three o'clock in the morning when I finally get back to the Valley. I stop at the twenty-four-hour newsstand on Van Nuys and Ventura and wait for the *L.A. Times* van to drop off a bundle of today's papers.

On the front page is a picture of Armani-man being lifted into an ambulance, his feet darting out from under a white blanket. Beside that photo is a picture of me taken in 1989 for my senior portrait. My hair is spiked in the front and I'm wearing this stupid gold necklace that my high school girlfriend gave me. I don't even think it was real gold. I always broke out in a thin red rash just under my Adam's apple whenever I wore the damn thing.

I look at the picture closely and see the rash. It's a reminder that my problems used to be significantly smaller.

The police think I murdered Pejman Barlavi with a kitchen knife found at the scene of the crime. My fingerprints are all over it.

The police know that I have robbed several restaurants in the greater Los Angeles area over the course of several weeks.

"Are you just gonna read that here," the newsstand attendant says, "or you planning on splurging for the quarter so you can take it home?"

I remember the morning I woke up at Claire's house and fixed myself a bagel. She set out the butter, the cream cheese, two onion bagels, a cutting board, and a sharp kitchen knife. I'd sliced myself a bagel, spread butter on it, and marveled at my incredible luck.

I look up and the attendant, who's got a copy of *Busty* sitting on his lap, is staring at me like I shot the President. "Sure," I say, handing him twenty dollars. "Give me all of them."

I park my car, with eighty copies of the *L.A. Times* stuffed into the trunk, two blocks from my apartment building. My foot feels like a hot brick, but since I've dumped out all my Vicodin, I limp along the entire way. I circle my building twice, looking for cops or anyone suspicious.

Not that I know what a suspicious person looks like. I've only seen them in movies, and they always look like Nick Nolte.

The only thing out of the ordinary is the guy doing laps around the building with one foot dragging behind him. I might as well have a hunchback, too.

Someone, probably my good friend Glen the building manager, has taped a notice to the front door of my apartment building, warning everyone about me. Old Glen got enterprising, it appears, and went into my apartment to find a picture of me to put on the bulletin. He chose a photo that'd been on my refrigerator since last Halloween. I'm dressed as a homeless person, so I have dirt smeared over my face and I'm wearing torn and ragged clothing. I'm also holding a sign that says, "Give Me Money or I'll Kill You." At the time, it got a lot of laughs.

What's nice about being a wanted man is that you are more likely to break lesser laws just because you can. For instance, I know that there is a restraining order against me right now and that by merely being at my apartment building I am in jeopardy of facing some real jail time plus a sizable fine. Not to mention that Glen might be inclined to attack me with whatever he's got in that little cave of an apartment he lives in.

But I know that my answering machine worked up until this evening. I think maybe Claire has left me a message. I think she has a plan already in motion and that all this worrying and running and dying is all just so much fuss.

It's not breaking and entering if you have a key, so I'm not in any real trouble when I walk into the lobby of my building—aside from that whole Glen business. Pencil me in for unlawful entry. Just add it to my file.

Breaking and entering can be added when I kick in the front door of my apartment.

My stuff is scattered everywhere. Just how I remember it.

I grab a green garbage bag from under the sink and fill it up with underwear, jeans, shoes, whatever clothes are left.

My computer is gone and my file cabinets are empty. It occurs to me that Glen probably wasn't the only person to look through my things. Maybe calling the police back today would have been a wise decision.

I stuff two boxes of Ritz crackers and a couple cans of sardines into the garbage bag before I finally stop long enough to play my answering machine.

Claire's voice floats into the room and I can feel her hanging in the air. When I hear her sweet breath tucked inside her words, I want to forgive her for everything. But I'm not that stupid anymore. Charity is approximate and imprecise, and my time of giving is over.

Claire says, "Lonnie."

I listen to her on the phone and I know that whatever has happened has already happened. She's talking into my answering machine because she already knows there's a dead man out there.

Claire says, "You've made a terrible decision."

At dinner, my mom told me I always had the best intentions when it came down to quashing reprehensible behavior in the people around me. Like in the Scouts, she said, when you quit after they wouldn't let that gay boy stay in. I didn't tell her that I quit because I was sixteen and tired of dressing up like I was playing Army.

Claire says, "You should have just left town. Why did you stand out there and watch him get wheeled away?"

I think about the night Claire and I went to Intermezzo. The way we disappeared through the crowded restaurant. I think about that day at McDonald's when she told me that parents need to care for their children.

Claire says, "I'm sorry, Lonnie, I really am."

Her voice falls from the air and shatters at my feet.

When catastrophe occurs, everyone always expects that there will be someone to chip in. Everyone always thinks the President will declare their bodies and minds "Disaster Areas" and will immediately begin making payments to ease the pain.

My body is not a building in Oklahoma City. My mind is not Northridge on a winter morning in 1994.

I know that whatever is in my apartment will be seized by the police, so I pull the tape out of my machine.

And then I stomp on it.

Then I melt it on my gas stove.

None of it works.

I can still hear Claire's voice.

I've got nothing but crap and it all fits in green garbage bags. I twist-tie everything. I grab a picture of my mom and one of Karen. There's a scrapbook I've always loved so it goes, too. It's like running out of a burning house. Everything you always loved must come out or sizzle like bacon. I take my Oakland A's baseball cap. I take my diploma from Cal State. My spices. Whatever will fit.

It's almost light out by the time I'm done.

My life is three green garbage bags with orange twist ties.

My life sits in the backseat of my Toyota Tercel. I sit in the front seat and do the only thing I can think to do.

I cry like a big fucking baby and then I get nauseated and I gag and I pound my fists on my thighs and the sun's coming up and I'm thinking, Screw Little Orphan Annie. What the hell does she know about the sun coming up?

When we were kids, Karen and I played a game on long car rides called "Would You Rather . . . " It was simple. Would you rather eat a cockroach or drink your own pee? Would you rather lick the toilet or kiss Great-Aunt Sadie?

Would you rather turn yourself in for a crime you didn't commit or flee from prosecution for a crime you did commit?

Karen could always justify her answers. Drinking your own pee can kill you, she would say. Eating a cockroach would suck for about ten seconds. Then it would just be another chewed-up piece of meat in your stomach. No harm, no foul.

Great-Aunt Sadie loves me, she'd say. If it makes her happy to cause me a little unhappiness, then so be it. She's gonna die soon anyway.

I never had Karen's ability to reason.

I'm driving on the 10 freeway toward Palm Springs. I'm 100 miles outside Los Angeles and I'm listening to a talk-radio program about me.

Bob from Duarte says, "You know, I saw this clown on the news this morning, you know that videotape they've been playing?"

The host, a guy who usually moderates a program about UFOs this time of the morning, says, "I saw that tape and it was just fascinating."

"Right," Bob from Duarte says. "So I say to myself, This guy, he's got some big ones, you know, because he's prancing around that house like he's King Tut or something. Fixing himself a bagel before he goes to slash up this poor guy. A real sicko, huh?"

"It makes me wonder if this is a man who equates food with sexual power," the host says.

"Right," Bob says. "Yeah, me too."

Kelly in Long Beach says, "First-time caller, longtime listener."

"Welcome," the host says. "We're talking about Lonnie Milton this morning. The founder of what is now being called 'Lonnie's Army' and the prime suspect in a bizarre murder. Go ahead, Kelly."

Lonnie's Army?

"Well, I saw this morning on *Urgent News* that they think this Lonnie guy has upwards of three hundred people working for him," Kelly says. "Like an entire militia. How long do you think he's been planning this assault on American commerce and do you think it is in any way related to alien abductions?"

"Absolutely," the host says.

"I mean," Kelly says, "if he's not involved with the Arabs."

"There is the whole matter of the dead Iranian man," the host says. "But it has long been my suspicion that the ancient societies of the Middle East are actually alien/human hybrids."

Before Kelly from Long Beach can answer, and before I gag again, I turn the radio off.

I've been out of Los Angeles for almost two hours. During that time I've made a few decisions. My first thought was to get out of the country, make a run for the border, and start a new life for myself in Mexico. I thought I'd live in a charming villa on the Sea of Cortez. I'd drink Corona all day and eat fish tacos all night.

Then I remembered that I wasn't in some John Grisham book. I hadn't just screwed the mob out of millions of dollars. No one was wiring me money to my offshore accounts in Grand Cayman and Saint Martin. In fact, I only have $823.12 in the bank.

Plus, I don't really like fish tacos.

My next decision was just to stay in L.A. I've seen all the specials on Discovery where people in the witness protection program move to Walla Walla or Poughkeepsie and are discovered mutilated days later. Or someone trying to avoid the law moves to a small Canadian town only to discover an old friend has moved in next door. Next thing you know, Robert Stack is broadcasting from your living room.

In L.A., I could grow a goatee, move out of the Valley, wait out my fourteen minutes and fifty-nine seconds of notoriety, maybe play some golf with O.J., and then make a big comeback somewhere around the year 2005, assuming there was a world to come back to.

But it's hard to do that when you have only $823.12.

Even harder when it's the last thing you want to do. I wanted to find Claire and clear what little of my name was left.

Palm Springs was an easy choice. No one goes to the desert in the summer. The streets would be empty, the hotels vacant. It would give me a chance to work out some things without worrying about the police.

But then I heard those two words that made me think that all of my plans meant nothing: Lonnie's Army.

I pull off the 10 in front of the Morongo Indian Bingo Casino, fifteen miles outside of Palm Springs. It's nine o'clock in the morning and the parking lot is filled with motor homes, buses, and Oldsmobiles. The transportation of the retired.

There are at least three hundred people inside playing bingo. Most of them are old women. They wear matching uniforms: floral print shirts, white pants, white shoes, golden dyed hair. Watching the festivities from every angle are hulking Indian men with .357s wearing Tribal Police uniforms.

The Tribal Police don't even glance at me. Then it occurs to me: I'm not even in America, technically. I'm standing in the middle of the Morongo Indian Nation.

I only had one real reason for stopping originally. The human bladder understands the fight or flight syndrome very well. If it knows the body is about to take flight, it decides when you need to travel a little lighter.

When I come out of the rest room, I see a bank of pay phones against the wall. I know my mom is having angina attacks right now. I know Karen is giving the news anchor on Channel 7 the eye. I know Julie is probably telling the world how she was my last lover and how special I was.

Mostly, I know that Charlie is sitting at his desk interviewing the unemployable.

I tell the Staff Genius receptionist that I'm interested in making an appointment for temp work. I tell her that I'm a college student on vacation and that I'll do anything. She asks my minimum salary request and I say the magic words that will get me transferred directly to Charlie:

"Five-fifty an hour is fine with me."

Charlie answers the phone just as he has been trained to by Corporate. Two rings. Sound stern. Sound rushed. "This is Charlie," he says. Except it sounds like THISISCHARLIE.

"Hi," I say. "I'm interested in working for the summer."

"What kind of skills do you have?" I hear Charlie lean back in his chair. He's been at work for three minutes and he's already getting comfortable.

"I know how to get into some really big trouble," I say. Charlie doesn't respond for almost a full minute.

"Well," he says evenly. "That's important to know."

"I didn't kill that guy," I say.

"Of course not."

"Are the police there?"

"No," he says, taking a deep breath. "You won't be required to work at home. Who really wants to have their personal life invaded?"

An old woman with a cane jumps up and screams, "Bingo! I've got Bingo!"

"I'm sorry," I say. "I never meant to drag you into this. Are you in any trouble?"

"Nothing to worry about," Charlie says. "If there's ever a problem with a job, all you need to do is call us and we'll take care of it. We're your security blanket. Think of Staff Genius as your own human resources department."

Charlie is reciting the Corporate script.

"Did my sister call you?"

"Your friend Karen referred you?" Charlie says. "She's a beautiful young lady. Quite a vision, really. I think she has the potential to be a very good worker."

Charlie wants to have sex with my sister.

"Great, Charlie, great," I say and then we both laugh. It is the first time I have done that in a very long time.

"Where the fuck are you?" Charlie whispers.

"The desert," I say.

"Your girlfriend just got done rolling over on you."

"Claire?"

"No, dumbass, Julie." Charlie's still whispering. "She just did an exclusive interview with Leeza Gibbons. Never trust a woman who smokes, man, they've got no fucking willpower."

"Where's she now?"

"Sitting in the conference room crying like Princess Di just died again," Charlie says.

"I need your help," I say.

"Why don't you call one of your three hundred minions," Charlie says. "Or I guess that should be amended to two ninety-nine."

"That's not funny."

"You're preaching to the converted," Charlie says. "I'm minion number one, my man."

"I need to find Claire," I say.

"I already did," Charlie says.

"What are you talking about?"

"ADP called today," Charlie says. "Said they were having trouble processing her paycheck because her social security number was wrong."

"Whose number was it?"

"Oh, it was Claire Gooden's," Charlie says. "Just not your Claire Gooden. This Claire had been dead for more than a year."

"That has to be a mistake," I say. "Can you run a background check?"

One of the main reasons large companies feel so safe using Staff Genius is our nationwide reputation for sending out only the finest temporary help. The way Staff Genius is able to confirm that an employee is trustworthy, honest, and qualified is through thorough background checking using all of the major reporting agencies. Staff

Genius considers Equifax and TRW partners in its quest to give excellent service to Fortune 500 companies. I know this is true. I've told clients the same thing, word for word.

"Yeah," Charlie says. "It'll take some time, though. If my buddy Dale is working at Equifax today, he's got that contact at the DMV who can get copies of all her records. You'll be breaking every stalking law on the books, so if it comes down, he doesn't know you. It's gonna be costly."

"How much?"

Charlie pauses and I can hear him tapping a pen against his teeth. "Case of beer," he says. "Maybe two."

"I can afford that."

"He might want first refusal on the script, also," Charlie says.

"What are you talking about?"

"Just thinking out loud," Charlie says.

I give Charlie all the information about Claire that I know, which is little. "I'm sorry," I say. "I don't know much about her aside from her name, I guess."

"This might not be the time," Charlie says, "but is your sister seeing anyone?"

"This isn't the time," I say.

"Right," Charlie says. "How do you want me to contact you when I get the information?"

"I'll call you," I say. "Or something. I don't know yet. I've got a feeling things are going to get pretty hot for you."

"Yeah," Charlie says. "What do you want me to tell your mom if she calls me again?"

"Nothing," I say. "And don't tell the cops anything either. I don't want you getting in trouble for harboring a known felon."

"Anything else before you go Richard Kimble on me?"

"See what you can find out about the dead Persian guy," I say. "I should at least be familiar with the person I supposedly killed."

"We keep track of your hours with our official Staff Genius time card," Charlie says, which means Julie must be done crying.

"I appreciate this, Charlie," I say.

"Tom Hanks plays me if this ever gets made," Charlie whispers and hangs up.

I sit in my car and listen to KFI News Radio and drink stale coffee out of a commemorative mug I purchased from the Morongo Indians for $3.95. I'm trying to figure out if it is safe for me to get on the road or if the CHP has snipers poised every five miles looking for me. What I learn is that the President thinks Iraq is being honest about its destruction of chemical weapons, the Spice Girls are making a new album, and I'm pretty much the next best thing to David Koresh.

Here is what I have learned about myself from the radio: I am in my mid-twenties. My high school algebra teacher remembers me as troubled but extremely bright. I recently tried to kill my landlord. My hatred for American commerce may be traced back to an early childhood experience when my mother was dating the head of Ronco. My father and I are very close and he just can't believe this is happening. My father blames my mother and says that she may be a lesbian. Julie, described as both "my lover" and "a close friend," considers me the greatest love of her life, a man who can be both charming and sinister, and someone who has the ability to become a chameleon. My sister has no comment. My mom has no comment. The CEO of Staff Genius released a statement to the media that said, in part, that as a member of the Staff Genius family I had always performed well. He also released a copy of the Wunderlich exam that I took prior to interviewing for my position. I scored a thirty-one, which means, he said, that I'm capable of doing any job. Lastly, a psychologist from UCLA says that my ability to mobilize such a large army of disciples suggests that I have a certain Hitler-esque quality. To lead so many down alleys of obvious misdirection, he says, shows that I am a rare form of sociopath.

Here are some of the statistics: 300-plus members of Lonnie's Army. More than 450 stolen meals. Two dead bodies, one an obvious murder. Millions in lost revenue for the city of Los Angeles. Three TV movies in the works. Upon my capture, feature film rights will be a hot commodity.

No mention of snipers, which is nice because I'm already on the road.

During my freshman year of college, I came to Palm Springs for spring break. I got drunk and acted stupid and threw up and then did it all over again. I brought the girl I was dating with me, but all she wanted to do was wear a thong bikini and ride on the back of a motorcycle down Palm Canyon. I wanted her to wear a thong bikini and walk down the street with me. This was back when Sonny Bono was still alive, still mayor, and still pissed off about people wearing thong bikinis downtown. It didn't matter. My girlfriend found some guy with long hair and a motorcycle and that was the last I saw of her until we got back to school.

Driving into Palm Springs now, though, is like cruising through a coal mine. I roll down my window and the air is so thick and hot that it feels like I'm breathing sulfur. The streets are vacant and silvery mirages hang just off the ground.

I'm tired. I've been awake for a month.

I park my car in front of a Motel 6 on Palm Canyon. I don't think I have enough energy to walk in and get a room, but I do it anyway. I don't want to boil alive in the front seat of my Tercel.

I tell the girl behind the counter that my name is Jake and that I need a room. I pay with cash. She says to me, "Can I see your driver's license, Jake?"

I can't help it. I'm so tired. I start to cry.

"It's okay," she says. "Really."

"I lost it," I say. I'm losing it.

"Okay," she says. No one likes to see a man cry. "No problem. There's no one staying here anyway."

"I'm an all-right guy," I say, not to the girl at the counter, really, but to myself. I say it to give myself a little push.

"I'm sure you are," she says, touching my hand. "Sir, it's going to be fine." She slides a key across the counter. "Everyone has days like this."

I flop onto the bed in room 243 of the Motel 6. I close my eyes and everything starts to swim in my head. Every little thing I've ever fucked up bubbles to the top of my mind.

Think about chemical warfare, I say to myself.

Let the light back in, Lonnie. Relax.

Think about making love beneath a tree.

Armani-man is calling my name.

Feet stick through a body bag.

Recite "The Concord Hymn" by Ralph Waldo Emerson. It's been stuck in the recesses of your mind since eighth grade, so you might as well use it.

I'm so tired of being tired.

I think of the last time I saw Claire. I think of how strangers always watched her. I think of the day she found me at Barnes and Noble.

I think how she's set me up.

Think about alien abductions.

Think about those poor Siamese twins.

Think about the world blowing up into a trillion tiny particles and you're just an atom floating through space. Let the light back in.

Find your own skin.

I wake up and it's morning. At first I think I haven't slept at all. It's not until I retrieve my complimentary copy of the *Palm Springs Desert Sun* newspaper that I'm absolutely certain that I have.

I'm not on the front page, which is a nice change. They have me on page three. There's no photo. There is, however, a graph detailing my activities over the course of the last forty-eight hours, including my lunch at Jerry's, my dinner at Mistral, and my appearance at the newsstand.

"He seemed pretty nervous," the night manager of the newsstand is quoted as saying. "I was afraid he was going to kill me."

I walk across Palm Canyon to a liquor store and use the pay phone in the parking lot to call Charlie. I tell the receptionist I'm a new client and that I've been referred to Charlie. He'll know it's me this way. No one ever refers clients to Charlie.

"Can you talk?" I say.

"Quickly," Charlie says. "The cops are in Julie's office."

"What did you find?"

"The only Claire Gooden on record with Equifax in Los Angeles County is the one who died last year," Charlie says. "And she was a he."

Fifteen

Claire Gooden was a sixty-five-year-old unmarried British man who died in 1998. His last known address was in Beverly Hills. He was worth several million dollars. He always paid his bills on time. Charlie said he had twenty-three credit cards. He also informed me that the world record for credit cards owned by one person was 1,216 with credit totaling $1.6 million.

What Charlie couldn't tell me was how Claire Gooden had died. I had a feeling it wasn't from natural causes.

"What are the cops doing there?" I ask.

"Getting ready to bug the place," Charlie says. "They brought all kinds of warrants with them and a bunch of electronic crap. They think Julie's been in contact with you."

"What about you?"

"They think I'm gay," he says. "I told them the only reason I let you sleep at my house was because I wanted to seduce you. Figured it might freak them out a little."

"Good idea," I say.

"Didn't stop them from parking in front of my building all night."

"What did you find out about the Persian guy?"

"Nothing," Charlie says. "The guy is clean. Just rich and dead."

"I need you to do one more thing for me," I say. "And then I understand if you want me to stop contacting you."

"I'm in for the long haul," Charlie says. "This is my ticket out of the temp business, my man. When this is done, I'm writing a screenplay."

"I need you to find out how Claire Gooden died," I say. "And find out if he left a woman a big hunk of money in his will."

"How am I supposed to do that?"

"You're the screenwriter," I say. "Do some research. If he died in California, it's all public record. Meet me at the Starbucks on Ventura and Kester tomorrow morning at seven."

"You think that's smart?"

"No one will recognize me," I say. "I've done this before."

I have a cab drive me out to the mall in Palm Desert. I've seen enough episodes of *The World's Dumbest Criminals* to know that I need to get rid of my car, and that using my credit cards or my ATM card will get me arrested pretty quickly.

I also know that by the time the police see that I used my ATM card in Palm Springs, I will be on my way back to Los Angeles. So I withdraw the maximum amount allowable from my checking account, exactly $500, from an ATM next to the mall's entrance. I make a point to smile into the camera above the machine.

I'm getting back to the basics. I'm firing it all back up again. I'm going to be Jake again because I need to be invisible. I'm going to recover what little of me is left. I'm going to find Claire, or whatever her name is, and I'm going to turn her over to the police. She's going to come clean and tell them that I'm only guilty of dining and ditching.

It's going to be my lifetime commitment. I'm going to fix everything. I'm going to get my couches back. I'm going to meet a nice girl and settle down.

And I'm going to tell the police about Bill Jennings. And I'll do time if I have to. Then I'll shed this Jake skin and show the world that Lonnie is decent. That this Lonnie's Army crap is just that: crap.

But first I need a new wardrobe.

I'm looking at a rack of rayon shirts in Macy's when a salesman walks up to me.

"Can I help you find something?" he asks.

"No," I say. "I'm just looking right now."

The salesman has deep blond hair and a perfect tan. He's wearing a dark blue suit with a silk tie. He smiles at me and I see that his right front tooth is chipped.

"It's okay," he says to me.

"What is?"

He looks over both shoulders and then back at me. "Just take it," he says. "Before the security guard comes back in this section."

"I have money," I say.

He laughs. "Mr. Milton," he says, and I see that he has a small cut above his lip, "we all *have* money."

"Do I know you?" I say, but I know the answer. I'm looking at minion number 152, head of the Palm Springs/Palm Desert/Coachella Valley chapter.

"Of course not," he says.

"How'd you get that cut?" I say, pointing to his face.

He runs his tongue over his upper lip and blushes. "Manager of Denny's," he says.

I step close enough to the salesman that I can smell his breath. He's breathing out of his mouth, almost panting. I see that there are thin beads of sweat on his nose. "I want you to do me a favor," I say. "I've got a gun in my pocket right now, and if you don't listen to me I'm going to stick it into your mouth and blow your tongue off. Are you following me?"

The salesman nods. His eyes are wide open. He's like a kid waiting in line at Disneyland for the first time.

"I want you to go into your manager's office after I leave and quit your job," I say. "And I want you to go home and call your mother or your father or whoever raised you and tell them that you love them and that you're sorry for being such a fuck-up. Okay?"

The salesman nods again.

"Say it," I say.

"Okay," he says. His voice is filled with excitement. "Yes, fuck yes, I'll do that."

"Then I want you to send that Denny's you ripped off some money for your meal, plus a tip," I say. "And if you don't do that, I'll know. I've got people all over this city and they've been watching your messy ass. Why do you think I'm here?"

"I've been careless," he says. "But that manager was strong. Broke my tooth. Did they see that?"

"You're out of my Army," I say, and the salesman bows his head. I catch my reflection in a mirror behind him and I can't believe what I see. My eyes are these tiny black gashes and my chest is all puffed out. There's a red tint to my face. I look like a bulldog.

"I'm sorry," he says.

"Give me your wallet," I say and he hands it to me. His license says his name is Jim Kochel. He's twenty-two. He lives in Rancho Mirage. He has fifty-three dollars and five different credit cards, all gold. There's a membership card for La Quinta Country Club. Jim Kochel is someone's bonus baby. Just killing time working at Macy's until the inheritance kicks in. He plays golf on the same course as Tiger Woods. He's got gold credit cards because Mom and Dad have million-dollar credit lines with 9 percent interest.

"You can take everything," he says. "Just let me stay in."

"Listen," I say, slipping his credit cards out of his wallet. "I'm not going to kill you, but we're watching you. I want you to go get a real job, something where you use your mind, all right? I don't ever want to see you working retail ever again. Do you know anything? Do you have any plans for the future?"

"My dad," he says, "owns a software company. That interests me. I could put a bug into one of the systems for you. I could do that. You know, I mean, whatever you want."

A security guard walks by and I step away from Jim Kochel, Lonnie's Army minion number 152.

"That's a good start," I say.

"I like origami," Jim says. "I've always liked art."

"Better," I say and Jim is beaming. "I'm taking your credit cards. Report them stolen in a week."

"Yes, sir," he says.

As I walk out of Macy's, I see Jim Kochel loosening his tie. He's getting ready to quit his job. Before I left him, he asked for my autograph. I signed the back of a Macy's gift certificate like I was Mark McGwire signing my seventieth home run ball: *Thanks for being such a great fan. We'll be watching you. Stop fucking up. Lonnie Milton.* And then I left with his five gold cards.

I buy two pairs of Armani slacks from a nice salesman at Nordstrom's who doesn't have any cuts on his face. The nice salesman points me toward the shoe department, where I purchase three pairs of Kenneth Cole shoes and five pairs of Calvin Klein socks.

I know. I'll never need this much stuff. The price is right.

I purchase four silk shirts, three sport coats, seven ties, and a bottle of cologne that comes in a container shaped like a man's body.

I spend $3,000 of Jim Kochel's credit at Nordstrom's.

Wilson's Leather is happy to sell me a lovely leather garment bag that comes with an eel-skin shaving kit.

"Be careful not to put any of your credit cards in the shaving kit," the salesgirl tells me. "Eel skin will deactivate the magnetic strip. And you wouldn't want to replace a gold card, right?"

"I've worked too hard for that," I say and then I wink. I've never winked at anyone in my entire life.

It's one o'clock. I have a whole new wardrobe. I have thousands of dollars worth of credit. I'm 130 miles from Los Angeles with no ride.

First I call the Motel 6 from a pay phone next to the mall bathrooms.

"This is Jake," I say when a man answers the phone. "I'm staying in your hotel."

"Your last name, sir?"

I look down at the bags scattered around my feet. "Nordstrom," I say. "Jake Nordstrom. I'm staying in room 243."

"I don't see your name here," the man says. "Are you sure you're calling the correct Motel 6?"

"I got in early yesterday," I say. "Maybe the girl at the front counter didn't mark me in."

"Impossible," the man says.

"Look," I say. "I know I'm staying there. Help me out here. Do you see a red Tercel in your parking lot?"

"One moment," he says and puts me on hold. Michael Jackson's "Billie Jean" comes on.

Two police officers walk out of the rest rooms and stand in front of the bank of pay phones I'm using. One has a mustache and the other is stocky and bald. They both have huge forearms.

"It's too goddamn hot," Mustache says.

"Could be worse," Stocky says. "We could be riding a horse in Central Park."

"It's cooler in Central Park," I say and both cops turn around. "Just got back from New York."

"No kidding," Mustache says. "What the hell you come here for?"

"I'm a heart surgeon," I say. "Big convention in town."

"No kidding," Mustache says. "What happened to your foot?"

"Polo," I say.

"I played some water polo," Stocky says. "Roughest sport there is."

"This was the horse variety," I say and both cops just look at me. "Billie Jean" turns into "I Can't Drive 55" by Sammy Hagar. "Any news on that lunatic in Los Angeles?"

"Just what you read in the papers," Mustache says.

"I guess you don't get much of that craziness here," I say.

"Oh, it's here," Stocky says. "We've rounded up a few splinters. They're just kids out here."

Sammy Hagar starts screaming about locking him up and throwing away the key because he just can't drive fifty-five. I'm talking about myself to two cops. I think the Motel 6 guy has forgotten about me.

I ask about violence. Is anyone getting hurt like that poor guy the other night?

Mustache kicks at his feet. Stocky fiddles with his nightstick.

"That was a real tragedy," Mustache says quietly and Stocky just bites his bottom lip.

"Well," I say, "you guys are just doing your job, right?"

"Right," Mustache says.

"Yep," Stocky says.

Write me up for ONE TWENTY-FIVE, Sammy Hagar sings, cuz I can't drive fifty-five!

"I can't save everyone I operate on," I say but the cops are already walking away.

I stand there for another three minutes and listen to Sammy Hagar break the law before the Motel 6 man picks me back up. "There is a red Tercel in our lot," he says, "filled with garbage bags. Is that yours?"

"Yes," I say. "I've had to fly out of town rather suddenly. I just don't want you to tow it away or anything."

"Mr. Nordstrom," he says, "we aren't a garage."

"Listen to me, you pompous fuck," I say because I just sweet-talked my way out of a potentially explosive, TNT-style blowup with two local cops and managed to make some rich kid give me all of his credit cards. "You're a two-bit employee of a Motel 6. You don't work for the Ritz-Carlton. You might as well be sitting on your ass inside a 7-Eleven making Slurpees. I'm leaving my fucking car there for a couple of days and you're going to watch it like it was the fucking Hope Diamond, or I'm going to come back and chop off your balls. Do we have an understanding?"

Silence.

The two cops are hassling a kid with a purple Mohawk standing outside Pacific Sunwear.

I'm sweating like a rabid dog.

My foot is throbbing.

There's a twenty-two-year-old kid standing in his manager's office in Macy's quitting his job and thinking about ways to install bugs in computer software with my autograph sizzling in his pocket.

Silence.

"I'll be back in a week," I say. "Ten days tops."

Silence.

"I could have you killed," I say because I could. I could go to Jim Kochel's house and tell him to kill whomever he finds working at the Motel 6 in Palm Springs.

A breath.

"That shouldn't be a problem, Mr. Nordstrom."

I sit in the backseat of a Mercedes-Benz limousine and drink Johnnie Walker Black on the rocks. I'm somewhere between Palm Springs and L.A.

I buzz the driver, Clyde, and ask him for the time.

"Two forty-five," he says.

I fiddle with the dial on my new Tag Heuer watch until the little hand is on the two and the big hand is on the nine. The Tag was my final purchase of the day. I didn't think my Casio digital did any justice to my improved wardrobe.

The limo was an afterthought.

Really.

I was going to take a bus into L.A., but then I remembered a documentary I saw on the Discovery Channel about the Night Stalker, Richard Ramirez. He took a bus back into Los Angeles after visiting his brother in Texas and the police had the entire depot staked out. He snuck out the back but ended up getting caught by locals on the street. They recognized Ramirez from his picture in the paper and beat the shit out of him.

So I started calling limo companies from the Yellow Pages until I found one that could take me back to Los Angeles. Clyde picked me up forty minutes later.

"You need anything back there, Doc?" Clyde asks. He thinks I'm a doctor, although I get the impression he calls everyone Doc.

"How do you get this TV to work?"

"The same remote you use for the stereo," he says.

I click on the TV and switch it to CNN. My old friend Bernard Shaw glares at me from his desk in Washington, D.C. He's talking about the Middle East. But really, Bernie is saying gather up your gold and silver, kiddies, the world's got about five more years until it implodes.

On MTV, Kurt Loder is interviewing Courtney Love about her new movie. Her right nipple hangs over the rim of her dress. Kurt is pretending not to notice.

I refill my drink.

On the WB, Buffy the Vampire Slayer is being interviewed on *Extra!* by Maureen O'Boyle. They never mention Buffy's real name. Under the actress's great big blond head and just above the Bebe label that's spread across her chest, the graphic says, "Buffy the Vampire Slayer."

"Looks like we're about to hit some trouble," Clyde says through the intercom.

"Cops?"

"Seems like it," he says. "Traffic's stopped in front of us."

I roll down my window and look outside. We're sitting still on the 10. I hear the sound of a helicopter overhead. I change the channel from Buffy to Channel 4 and there I am.

Or, rather, there we are.

"Colleen," the reporter inside the helicopter says, "you're absolutely right. This is domestic terrorism. By doing this here, they are, in effect, shutting down the main artery between Los Angeles and Palm Springs."

There are three cars on fire in the middle of the 10 freeway.

Going both directions.

"What's your sense of the mood on the freeway, Steve?" Colleen says.

"There's a lot of agitated drivers," Steve, the voice in the sky, says.

I roll up the window and take a sip of my drink.

"What's the news say, Doc?"

"Domestic terrorism," I say.

I switch over to Channel 5 because I know they have the Urgent News Apache fighter helicopter, and hit the mute button.

There's a Ford Explorer. A Honda Civic. A school bus. They're all on fire.

The camera pulls back and shows traffic jammed for miles in each direction.

An Impala. A Cadillac. A garbage truck.

"Like Arabs or something?" Clyde asks.

"Like Oklahoma City," I say.

Someone is in charge.

You can't blow up a garbage truck without some direction. A school bus takes some initiative, too.

"We're living in a crazy time, Doc."

I down my drink and pour another. And another. I drink until I can't feel my face; until I can pinch my left eyeball and it doesn't even faze me.

I change the TV back to CNN and Bernard Shaw is pissed at me. He levels his eyes and starts talking. You little punk, he's saying, like I don't have enough to worry about? Like that nut in Iraq isn't making weapons of mass destruction *right now?* Remember that guy from the eighties in Libya? He's making a comeback, too. And you, Bernie's saying, you've gotta stick your rotten nose into my holocaust? This is my time, buddy. I've got my own career to think about, you know, and you're strictly local news.

Shaw's face evaporates and there we are again. A sea of unmoving cars parted by yellow flames and black smoke.

The screen splits and on one side is Bernie and on the other there's just a burning school bus.

"Doc," Clyde says. "They're saying on the radio that people are hurt up there."

I'm disappointed in you, Bernie is saying.

"You think we should try to drive up on the shoulder so you can see if you can help?"

Little kids, Bernie says.

"No," I say.

"But Doc," Clyde says, "the radio says people could be dying."

"I'm not a doctor like that," I say. "I'm a teacher."

Bernard Shaw disappears, replaced by a commercial for tampons. I turn the sound back on.

"Who'd do something like this?" Clyde says.

"Everyday people," I say.

"Doesn't anybody have any sense of rules?" Clyde says.

"Maybe they've lost hope," I say.

Like any of us can be saved.

Bernard comes back on so I switch back to Channel 4.

Hello, Julie.

She's wearing the same dress she wore to Bill Jennings's funeral. The same dress I pushed over her hips when we fucked up against her dishwasher.

"I don't think he's capable of organizing something this large," Julie says. She's standing in the lobby of Staff Genius. The couches are full of applicants. I can see three people taking typing tests. Business is booming.

"Now we understand that Mr. Milton is in the Palm Springs area," the reporter interviewing Julie says. "Did you two ever share any special memories in the desert?"

"We never made the time," Julie says.

The reporter turns to the camera and purses his lips. "Time," he says. "Something Lonnie Milton will be doing a lot of. For Channel 4, this is Mark Hernandez reporting live from Century City."

There are a hundred things I haven't had time for in my life.

I always wanted to play the guitar.

I wanted to go to the gym more often.

I wanted to have a dog.

I never, ever, wanted my life encapsulated by a woman I fucked when I was stoned on Vicodin.

Sixteen

The limo driver, Clyde, wakes me up. "Doc," he says. "I got us some cheeseburgers."

I sit up and look at my watch. It's 4:30.

"What happened?"

"You passed out," Clyde says, handing me a quarter pounder with cheese before he sits down beside me. There's an empty bottle of Johnnie Walker on the floor. "I locked up and walked back to the last exit."

The TV is still on. Channel 4 has stopped its wire-to-wire coverage of people sitting on the 10. Rosie O'Donnell is interviewing the Backstreet Boys.

"Any idea when we're gonna get moving again?"

"CHP rolled by and said they'd be able to open up a lane around five o'clock," Clyde says. "You wanna stand up and stretch your legs while you still got a chance?"

I roll down the window. People sit on the hoods of their cars. Children run from one side of the freeway to the other. They are actually playing in traffic.

There are so many helicopters in the sky that it looks like the day they airlifted the Americans out of Saigon.

"I'll stand up when we get to L.A.," I say.

Clyde smiles. "Saw you on TV," he says.

One.

Two.

Three.

Now take a breath.

Good.

Smile. Try to blush.

"I didn't think anyone watched PBS anymore," I say.

"Doc," Clyde says, chewing his burger. "We're both stuck here, right?"

My head feels like it is dissolving and inflating at the same time. I can reach down and grab the empty bottle of Scotch and belt Clyde in the face if I have to because right now nothing matters.

"I don't make up the rules," I say. The bottle is about a foot away

from me.

"Who does?" Clyde asks. "We're just two guys sitting in a limo eating some burgers."

"You're the boss here," I say. "I'm just trying to get home."

"News said that school bus was empty," Clyde says. "But that it was filled with mannequins and stuffed animals."

The Backstreet Boys and Rosie O'Donnell are singing a song together. The audience is going wild.

"That's a pretty sick trick," Clyde says and stuffs a handful of fries into his mouth.

"I didn't have anything to do with that," I say. If I have to hit Clyde, I'll have to kill him. He's a big man, maybe 250 pounds, and there's deep scar tissue around both of his eyes. His nose is flat like a boxer's.

Outside, a little girl is jumping rope in the number 4 lane of Interstate 10.

"Of course not," Clyde says. "You're like the President. You don't get your fingers dirty, right?"

"I'm nobody," I say. "I work for an employment agency. I make less than thirty thousand a year."

"David Koresh, what was he?" Clyde says. "Thought he was a rock star or something. But you're the real deal, Doc. You dress like a violent Tony Robbins and everything." There's a ringing sound and Clyde reaches into the inside pocket of his jacket and pulls out a cell phone. He lays it between us.

Ring.

"Are you going to answer that?" I ask.

"You gonna hit me with that bottle?"

I look down at the empty bottle of Scotch and then back at Clyde. He's got this look on his face that isn't angry or anxious or even funny. It's just a look that says he's been in situations far tougher than this one.

"Are you going to turn me in?"

Ring.

Ring.

"I don't care about politics, you know?" Clyde says. "I drive from point A to point B and then I go home and watch TV or have a beer with my ex-wife. Pretty simple, right?"

Ring.

"I can pay you," I say.

Ring.

"I saw that school bus on fire and I wanted to kill whoever did that," Clyde says. "Kids don't know a goddamn about anything. They just like bees, you know?"

Ring.

"They just nervous energy all bundled up," Clyde says. He's starting to breathe heavily. "And if you killed some kids just for nothing, I'd, well, I wouldn't be able to understand that. I'm not a violent man, Doc."

Ring.

"I didn't kill any kids," I say. There's a vein in Clyde's forehead that's pulsing. His hands are clenched so tightly that his thumbs are twitching.

Ring.

"Ever?"

Ring.

I lean forward until Clyde and I are almost nose to nose.

I'm way past the point of rational thought.

People would rather be scared than dead.

"Never children," I say.

Ring.

"Only men."

Clyde reaches for the phone and I put my hand over his.

"And if I'm arrested or hurt or something goes wrong in here," I say, "then you're responsible, Clyde. And they know where I am."

I move my hand and Clyde answers the phone.

I sit back and try to make my face look narrow and long. I imagine I'm James Coburn. I imagine I'm one of those tough guys in mobster movies. I'm James Caan in *The Godfather.*

"Sorry, Boss," Clyde says into the phone, "I'm stuck on the 10."

I nod my head.

Good.

Long, narrow.

"All right," Clyde says and hangs up.

"That was good," I say.

Clyde grabs me by the throat and squeezes.

"Don't you ever threaten me," he says.

I'm in the Caldecot Tunnel.

"I'm not one of your little terrorists," he says.

I'm at Bill Jennings's funeral.

"We got a working agreement here," he says.

My plane has crashed. I'm floating underwater.

"I don't want your money or anything," he says.

I'm in bed with Claire. She's looking down at me and I'm right there. I'm right there.

"Cops pull us over, I don't know a damn thing," he says. "They wanna take you out of the car and beat you like a piñata, that's not my problem."

I'm in seventh grade. Nicole Nickerson is sucking on my ear.

"We clear?"

I nod my head and all I see are stars.

Orion's Belt.

The Big Dipper.

Clyde lets go of my throat.

The sun. Nothing but the sun.

"I'm sorry," I try to say, but nothing comes out.

I open my eyes and Clyde hands me a McDonald's napkin. "Wipe your face," he says. "You got slobber all over yourself."

I sit there for a long time and don't say anything. I think about my mom and how she's probably scared to death. I think about my sister and how she's always tried to save me and about how hopeless she must feel. I think about Charlie and about sacrifice. I think about my dad and about Julie and about all those people on TV who know me, I mean *know me:* the psychologists, the doctors, the experts, the man on the street with an opinion.

I think about this world I've created. About how, no matter when this ends, it will never end. That when I'm sitting in a jail cell or when some cop has a gun to my head and I'm telling him to just shoot, it will still be going on. There will be the articles in the newspaper, the stories on *20/20,* my family, my friends, the people I've met—the Clydes of my world—who will live these moments in perpetuity.

And there is Claire, I suppose.

And where am I in all of this? Where am I when this is all over? A token for Claire. An instrument in whatever game she was playing? A willing participant in something so pitiless.

In the end, there won't be the slightest sense of me left. A cruel joke about fame.

"Looks like things are starting to move," Clyde says. He's sitting up front again, but he's lowered the window between us.

"Why are you doing this?"

"I don't believe in you," Clyde says. "I don't think you're really sitting in the back of my limo planning to blow up the world."

Fake. Liar. Cheat.

"So I'm not real?"

"Not like they say on the news." Clyde presses a button and the tinted window between us slides back up.

We snake by the burnt-out hulls of the cars. There are dozens of cops, plus men and women in black suits. I think they must be FBI agents because whenever I've seen FBI agents on TV, they're always wearing black suits.

In the back of one of the police cars, two men are sitting side by side. I wonder who they are and why they've done this. I wonder if they know that they are ruining themselves for someone like me.

It's not like they've blown up cars for Michael Jordan or Elvis or even Jesus. They've done it for a picture in the newspaper. A story on the local news. An ideal I don't even believe.

Two guys are sitting in the back of a squad car and they're probably talking about me. About how proud of them I must be. They think I'm free. They think I've made my escape and now I can control my empire from atop the Sierra Nevada mountains or my compound in the Cascades.

So we're back to where we started: We're on the freeway and we're flying through the Inland Empire. We're passing motor homes and taxicabs and Pathfinders and motorcycles.

We pass Fontana, Upland, Pomona. We pass the Sizzler. McDonald's. Circuit City. Colton Piano.

We pass the Nike Superstore and the Reebok Outlet Center.

We climb over the foothills and into downtown Los Angeles as the last strands of daylight fade. Billboards tell me that a trip to the Body Shop will give me the smell of compassion. 92.3 FM will erase all color lines. Pepsi will give me youthful vitality. Commissioner Cook will be tough on crime. The Gap will give me the identity I need and want. Nike, the all-knowing Nike, the all-fearing, all-loving, all-the-clothes-I'll-ever-need Nike, tells me Just Do It.

Every brand must have an identity.

The billboard that bears my face hangs over the Melrose Boulevard exit off the 101. It says that I am wanted for murder and mayhem. Across the center of my chest, an enormous Staff Genius logo is fixed above an italicized string of words: *This billboard paid for and endorsed by the Staff Genius family. Building balanced workers for tomorrow's communities!*

In this time of compassion we're living in, when it is America's duty to save the world, business has finally replaced civil society. And I'm Jerry's Kid for the year.

"Where am I dropping you?" Clyde asks after we've passed the billboard.

"I don't know," I say. "Can we just drive for a little while?"

Clyde rolls down the window between us.

I'm trying not to cry again because I told myself to be a man and take care of business.

I'm trying.

"Sure, Doc," Clyde says. "Sure."

133

Clyde parks the limo in front of the Chateau Marmont on Sunset.

"Isn't this where Belushi died?" I ask.

"No one will bother you here," Clyde says. "They won't even look twice at you."

I step out of the limo while Clyde pulls my bags from the trunk. There's a black Ferrari parked next to a red Viper. A white Rolls idles in the driveway.

"Give me one of your credit cards," Clyde says.

"Take all of them," I say and hand him my wallet.

"I told you I don't want your money," Clyde says. "People who show up at this place in a limo don't go in and register like normal folks. Wait here for a minute."

I stand outside and watch Clyde walk into the lobby. He could be going inside to call the police, but I know he's not. I know because I still remember what it was like to be a normal person.

Across Sunset, people wait to get into Dublin's. The sun has only been down for thirty minutes and already there are women in skintight black dresses waiting to be noticed by the guys in baggy silk pants and shiny silver shirts.

If I could see what was happening three blocks away, I'm sure I'd see the *Dawson's Creek* crowd gathering in front of the House of Blues. One more block and I'd see my friend the Los Angeles Laker striding through the unluckies waiting for an invitation into Sky Bar.

A block south and I'd see the tan boys in tight shirts.

One more block, hookers and their johns.

Two more, fashionable ex–punk rockers would be dining on an expensive Italian dinner before checking out what was in stock at Aardvarks.

Ten more, poor Mexican families.

Twelve, blacks.

Twenty-five and I could see hookers again.

"No problems," Clyde says and hands me my wallet and a room key.

"Who do they think I am?"

"Jim Kochel," Clyde says. "Whoever that is."

"He's still alive," I say. "Just unemployed."

Clyde frowns and sucks in his cheeks.

"I'm just trying to recover my satellites," I say. "Whatever I can salvage."

"Don't hurt anybody else," Clyde says.

"I'm trying," I say. "I don't have control over any of this."

"You're all right with me," Clyde says. "But I think you're all kinds of mixed up."

Every girlfriend I've ever had has told me I need to share my feelings.

My sister believes I should meditate.

Charlie thinks I need anger management classes.

"I appreciate that, Clyde," I say.

"Tell me something, Doc," Clyde says. "You really kill that Persian guy?"

"No," I say.

Bill Jennings.

Armani-man.

The Persian's name was Pejman Barlavi and he is dead.

I must find out Armani-man's name.

"I've never killed anyone."

Clyde tips his cap to me and I wonder why I need to lie to him. Why not tell him that people are dying all around me and that he should watch his ass?

I wave to Clyde as he backs the Mercedes-Benz limousine onto Sunset Boulevard. From behind my gritted teeth, I say, I'm sorry I lied to you. I say, Thank you for not believing in me. I say, Tell everyone you know that Claire was beautiful and I was desperate. Tell them that everything was moving so quickly and that everything trembled. I say, Tell them that when I think about her she looks blurred around the edges, like some kind of dream. But tell them I'm going to find her and I'll stop spinning and I'll make the right choices and that I'm going to keep on living and I'm going to keep on fighting and I'm not going to hurt anyone else.

Clyde doesn't wave back, but I think he hears me.

Seventeen

The Channel 4 anchorwoman, Colleen, is flirting with me.

She tells me she's forty-seven years old.

Not to worry, she also informs me, because she doesn't mind younger men.

She's downing chocolate martinis like they're lemonade.

"Have you ever filmed yourself?" Colleen asks.

We're inside Rix. I found her sitting at the bar.

"No," I say. "I don't like to leave any evidence."

Colleen laughs and squeezes my forearm.

"Are you sure you don't live here?" she asks.

I order Colleen another drink.

"I live in Texas," I say. "I'm in real estate."

It's nine o'clock and this is the fourth restaurant I've been into. My hair is slicked back and I'm wearing sunglasses, even though it's night. If Jack Nicholson can do it, Jake can do it for an evening.

"I work in entertainment," Colleen says.

"Adult?" I say.

Colleen tips her head back and shrieks with laughter. There are scars where her jaw meets her neck. I think she may actually be fifty-seven.

"You're a doll," she says. "I'd love to experience you."

The crowd at Rix is older and wealthier than where Claire and I usually went. But I figure she's on the prowl for another rich man. Except she's not here.

"I'd like that," I say, "but I'm flying back to Houston tonight."

Colleen, the woman who referred to me as a "domestic terrorist" earlier in the day, writes her phone number on a napkin. "Call me when you get back," she says.

I take a lap through the restaurant before I leave and I see a woman who sells infomercial products on late-night TV eating a lamb shank. I also see half of the cast of *Friends* sitting in a dark booth.

There are so many stars in all of these places, so many significant people, that I merely melt into the framework. I can go into any place, any room, and all anyone will see is a well-dressed man. A single satellite in a galaxy of burning suns.

I prove it in restaurant after restaurant.

The maitre d' at Chinois greets me like we are old friends.

The bartender at Reign buys me my drink.

I sit next to Richard Grieco at Le Dome and talk about baseball.

At Morton's, at Spago, at Da Pasquale, at Rebecca's, at La Boheme, at Ivy, I search for her and nobody looks at me with a crossed eye.

I have conversations with people I have never met. I share a drink with a teenage girl who tells me she's on TV, and aren't I? Yes, I say. Yes.

A cabdriver tells me he's seen it all, but that this bullshit with the free dinners is killing L.A. "Worse than Rodney King and O.J. combined," he says.

When the restaurants close, I hit the bars.

The Gate. Sky Bar. Liquid Kitty. Lava Lounge. Century Club.

In every bar, in every drink I swallow, in every hour that drips by, I know that Claire is slipping farther and farther from my grasp.

I follow a couple into a bar called Coach and Horses because the girl looks like Claire from behind. It's not her, I know, but I sit and watch the couple slobber drunk kisses on each other for the next twenty minutes anyway. I'm doing it because I can't think of what else I can possibly do.

Because it's one forty-five in the morning and I'm running out of choices.

Because there's a knife with my fingerprints on it.

Because there's a movement with my name attached to it.

It's like a game of hide-and-go-seek and the only person still hidden is myself.

"Last call," the bartender says.

I'm in a filthy bar in Hollywood watching a girl who looks like Claire lick some guy's neck.

"Last call," the bartender says again.

Yes, I think, it is.

Eighteen

Armani-man's name was Todd Harris. He was nineteen, a freshman at UCLA, a promising track star in high school before he tore his anterior cruciate ligament during his senior year, and he's being buried today at noon in ceremonies being held at Forest Lawn Cemetery.

I learn this reading the *L.A. Times* while sitting in the backseat of the Chateau Marmont's personal limousine. It's six-thirty in the morning and I'm on my way to meet Charlie at Starbucks.

The *Times* is also reporting that I am believed to be on my way to Nevada, where sources indicate I have a large and loyal following.

All of this information is found on page three. Pages one and two are devoted to color photos of a burning school bus and stalled traffic. Pages four through eight are a special pullout section devoted solely to my alleged crimes, including a complete timeline from the date of my birth to today.

The two men arrested at the scene of the fire claimed their names were Lonnie Milton.

I haven't heard my own name in days.

"Where do you want me to drop you, Mr. Kochel?" my driver asks. We are half a mile from Starbucks.

"Just let me out here," I say.

"Do you want me to wait for you?"

"No," I say.

Seven years?

Twenty years?

Life?

Lethal injection?

"I don't know how long I'll be," I say.

I walk west down Ventura and think that I need to remember what it feels like to be free.

I need to remember that even if this all turns out okay, I'll never be manager of the Encino branch of Staff Genius.

I'll never buy anything at IKEA and attach any importance to it.

I'll never wish I were famous.

Or noteworthy.

Or dangerous.

I'll never say, "I'll never."

I stand across the street from Starbucks and watch Charlie. He's sitting by himself at a table outside, a briefcase at his feet. I wait until everyone who arrived at the same time as Charlie leaves before I cross the street.

Not that I think they would recognize me.

I'm wearing black pants, a cream-colored silk shirt with a matching tie, and a black sport coat. I threw my sissy boot away this morning so that I could cram my broken foot into a pair of Kenneth Cole shoes; consequently I'm also sporting a limp.

I have on a pair of wraparound black sunglasses and I've combed my hair forward so that my bangs hang to my eyebrows. I look like your garden-variety asshole who goes to Starbucks every morning.

Charlie is reading the paper when I sit down across from him.

"Sorry," he says, "but I'm straight."

"It's me," I say and tilt up my glasses.

"I knew that," Charlie says.

"Anyone follow you this morning?"

"No," Charlie says. "I think they're all on their way to Nevada."

"I don't know where they get this stuff," I say.

"Nice job on the freeway system," Charlie says. "Took me three hours to get home."

"Did you get what I asked for?"

"Talked to your sister last night," Charlie says, opening up his briefcase. "We're having dinner after you get arrested."

"How's my mom?"

"Sedated," Charlie says and slides a manila envelope across the table.

"I'll open this later," I say.

"You'll want to open it now," Charlie says. "She's in there."

There are at least twenty people sitting outside drinking coffee. I look at each one of them, trying to see if they are watching me.

I try to find unnatural bulges around ankles or under arms.

I listen for approaching sirens and the *whoop-whoop* of helicopter blades.

"Go ahead," Charlie says. "I'll keep a lookout."

I rip open the envelope and start reading.

Her name is Hillary Peck and she's about to be very wealthy.

Again.

Claire Gooden was killed by a stab wound to the throat inflicted by a twenty-seven-year-old man named David Ruttenburg, who's now serving twenty-five to life at Chino.

Other than several charities, the only beneficiary of Mr. Gooden's estate was Hillary Peck.

There's a copy of a California driver's license for Hillary Peck.

Her hair is blond.

Claire's hair is brown.

Her eyes are blue.

Claire's eyes are green.

Her skin is golden and her lips are parted just enough so that I can see the bottom of her two front teeth.

"Where did you get this?" I ask, holding up the photocopy.

"You owe my buddy Dale at Equifax and his Deep Throat at the DMV a keg of beer," Charlie says.

Men are dead and all I'm thinking about are the moles around her clavicle.

My life is ruined and all I can do is stare at a frozen picture.

I'm in control.

I'm in control.

"Heads up," Charlie says.

There's a woman in a Starbucks uniform walking toward our table holding two large cups of coffee. Her eyes are fixed on me.

"Here's your coffee, sir," she says, placing the drinks in front of

me.

"I didn't order anything," I say.

"Of course not," she says.

I'm in control.

"Would you like a pastry?" she asks.

I have Claire in my hands. I. Am. In. Control.

"A scone maybe?" she says. "How about some lemon bundt cake?"

"I'm not who you think I am," I say.

"Of course not, Mr. Kochel," she says and walks away.

Think about that girl in the well.

Think about Armani-man, Todd Harris, bleeding in the street.

Think about David Ruttenburg doing life.

Think about Claire Gooden, the real Claire Gooden, getting a knife in the throat.

"We are not the droids you're looking for," Charlie says.

Another Starbucks employee, a male, sets an entire coffee cake on our table.

"I need to get out of here," I say.

"You never told me about all this free stuff," Charlie says, slicing a piece of cake. "There are some perks to being a misunderstood criminal genius. That's what they're calling you, by the way."

"I've heard," I say.

Charlie raises his cup of coffee and shakes it in the air, just like Claire used to do when she wanted more wine. A Starbucks drone swoops down and replaces it with another frothy cup.

"I need to borrow your car," I say.

"Impossible," Charlie says.

I slide Jim Kochel's American Express Gold Card across the table. "Rent a limo for the day. Fly to Aruba. Whatever."

Charlie looks at the card and smiles. "I could take your sister to a really nice place with this."

"Is there more information on Hillary Peck in here?" I ask, holding up the envelope.

"Everything I could find," Charlie says. "What are you going to do?"

"I'm going to find her."

"And what? Get yourself killed?" Charlie leans forward and grabs my hand. "This is stupid, Lonnie. Take this to the police and come clean for what you did do. They don't have any proof about this terrorism crap, right?"

"It's not that simple," I say. "I was in that house. My fingerprints are on the knife that killed the Persian guy."

Pejman Barlavi.

Say his name.

"Pejman Barlavi," I say.

"What are you going to accomplish by finding her?"

"I don't know yet," I say.

Charlie lets go of my hand and rubs his forehead. I've never seen Charlie angry, really angry, or sad for that matter. Until now.

"Lonnie," Charlie says finally, "I care about you. We're friends, right?"

"You're my only friend," I say.

"Then do me a favor," he says. "Don't end up in Forest Lawn out of pride. Find this girl, get whatever evidence you need, and go to the police."

"I will," I say.

Charlie gazes down into his coffee for a minute and I think that I'm lucky to have someone like him. Someone who is willing to risk everything for a friend, even when he knows his friend is wrong.

"There's something else." Charlie raises his head slowly. "I've been promoted."

"Did you get my Encino office?"

"Worse," Charlie says. "Corporate came in yesterday and fired Julie."

Charlie is now Management.

"Handed me a bunch of buttons, a few logo pens, a twenty-five percent raise, and said get to work," Charlie says. "So, you've still got a job if you need one."

"I appreciate that," I say. "But I won't be coming back."

Charlie fishes his car keys from his pocket and slides them across the table. "I just got that smell out," he says. "It's parked in the back."

"I'll be gentle with it," I say and Charlie and I both stand up.

I want to tell Charlie not to worry about me. I want to tell him that although our worlds have turned upside down, I'm still the same. There are a lot of things I want to say to Charlie because I know it's going to be a long time before I see him again.

I tell him about Bill Jennings.

I tell him about Armani-man.

I tell him that all I ever wanted was to have a new life.

I tell him that he should quit his job at Staff Genius, that he should find something he really loves doing and then he should do it.

I tell him that maybe all of this happened for a good reason, maybe I was meant to suffer so that I could appreciate everything I never had, never did, made excuses for.

I tell him that my mother always thought I was self-destructive and that she was probably right.

I tell him that my sister is a nice girl and that they might make an attractive couple.

I tell him that even if I end up doing 100 years in prison, at least I know that someone was looking out for me and that someone was concerned about me and that someone never stopped believing in me.

"Don't trash my car," Charlie says because he's crying and isn't used to showing any kind of real emotion. "It's not paid for."

Nineteen

I sit in my room at the Chateau Marmont and read pages of documents culled from the DMV, the reporting agencies, and the Internet.

It occurs to me while I read about this woman who was Claire to me, this Hillary Peck, that she knew long ago what it meant to feel irrelevant.

A high school education, two years at Los Angeles Pierce Community College, and short stints at several jobs, including Ruby's Diner, Clothestime, Wet Seal, and Wicks N' Sticks.

She is thirty-three years old and has never been employed for more than two months at a time. In Staff Genius lingo, Hillary Peck is an unhireable.

Who needs to have a job when you can latch on to a millionaire and then have someone kill him?

Who needs to learn how to type when you can make an executive want to leave his wife?

David Ruttenburg, the man who "killed" the real Claire Gooden, worked at Century Insurance, according to a newspaper article from the *Orange County Register*'s web site. A model employee, the story said. A real up-and-comer, his manager said. His only previous brush with the law was a minor shoplifting incident two months previous. A good thing, the police said, or else they never would have had his prints on record.

I'm sure it was the only time he ever shoplifted.

I'm sure that when David Ruttenburg was stuffing steaks or lamb chops down his pants, there was a very pretty woman with him.

So that's how she does it regularly. We just never got caught.

My apartment was robbed so that the police would have a copy of my prints. Beating up Glen was a bonus.

David Ruttenburg plea-bargained down to second-degree murder, what with his previous clean record and all, and is still doing twenty-five to life.

I've assaulted a man.

I've robbed restaurants.

I've killed a man.

I've masterminded domestic terrorism.

They're going to stick me in a tub full of water, then they're going to throw in a fully operational electric generator. It will be a pay-per-view event.

Hillary Peck was so irrelevant that she lived in the same apartment in West Los Angeles for three years. She had five credit cards: JCPenney, Sears, Macy's, Texaco, and American Express.

Her Wells Fargo MasterCard account was canceled with her owing $2,700.

Her Bank of America Visa was canceled with her owing $3,600.

Hillary Peck has been turned over to eleven collection agencies since her eighteenth birthday.

Hillary Peck was so irrelevant that she simply reinvented herself. She put on a skin of wealth and prosperity and wore it like a mink coat. She found rich, lonely men and drank their wine and licked their necks and did things to them that they'd only read about in nature magazines.

And if she couldn't get any more money from them? She found someone just as irrelevant as she was, and then she gave them a life.

Gave them a new identity and a taste of what she had. And when it was time, when she had weaseled her way into money, or power, or whatever it was she needed, she took her Mr. Relevant's life and blamed it on her current Mr. Irrelevant.

Here comes the dread and nausea.

Here comes I'm sick of the wallowing.

Here comes a garlic taste in the back of my throat that I've always associated with revenge.

Everything Claire did, she did out of habit. There were no new steps.

I've been looking for Claire in all of the wrong places.

She's not looking for a wealthy man. Not yet at least.

Right now, Claire is looking for a young man. She is looking for someone who is between twenty-five and twenty-nine, I think. A man who looks as if his greatest thrill in life was when he stole a box of pens from his office.

The model applicant should look pretty good in a shirt and tie because he'll need to dress up.

He should be able to "think outside of the box," as Corporate Staff Genius liked to say.

He doesn't need to be funny or look like Tom Cruise, but it would help if he were able to hold intelligent conversation with complete strangers and have some ability with the opposite sex.

Claire isn't slipping in and out of fancy restaurants because none of the candidates for her job opening can afford to hang out in those places.

Think, Lonnie.

Think.

I call the front desk and ask if they can send up as many area phone books as they can spare. I'm especially interested in the San Fernando Valley, West Los Angeles, and the beach cities. Ten minutes later, a bellboy hands me six phone books.

When Julie was out with the shingles, Charlie and I devised a drinking game involving the files of our Staff Genius applicants. Charlie would read the applicant's name and address and I would have to guess their yearly income. It got to the point where we were both able to look at someone's résumé and based solely on his address, decide whether or not he was lying on his application about his actual net worth.

It takes me almost two hours, but I draw a rude map of my target income areas.

There are fifty-six major bookstores between Woodland Hills and Marina Del Rey. Thirty-seven of them have either a Starbucks or a Starbucks rip-off within a hundred yards of their front doors; the other nineteen have them inside their front doors.

It is eleven-thirty in the morning and for the first time in my entire life, I know exactly what I'm doing.

Her name is Hillary Peck and I'm going to catch her.

I start in Marina Del Rey and work my way north.

I expect that Claire's hair will be shorter and lighter, her eyes will be an entirely new shade, and that she will be driving a different car.

In all the information that Charlie and his friends at Equifax were able to get, there was nothing about Pejman Barlavi. He was younger than the real Claire Gooden for sure, and when I saw him he didn't look particularly lonely. So why had she picked him to kill?

I will ask her that before I call the police.

I wade through stacks of books at Dutton's, Book Soup, and forty-two other large, warehouse-style stores without seeing Claire.

What I do see are all of the candidates. They wear white T-shirts with sweater vests, Gap jeans, and Nike Air Jordans. They read *Adweek, Electronic Media, Spin,* and *ESPN: The Magazine.* They wear blue shirts with red ties, gray slacks, and black loafers. They read *GQ, Vanity Fair, Omni,* and *Golf Digest.*

They drink nonfat, no whip, venti mochas.

Nonfat venti lattes with a shot of espresso.

They drive Honda Accords, Toyota Camrys, Volkswagen Jettas, and on the rarest of occasions, motorcycles.

And any one of them could be looking at serious time if he's not careful who he spills his coffee on.

The women in the bookstores are all the same, too. None of them have Claire's electricity. I make eye contact with several attractive women, and they all turn their heads away. Claire would have held my gaze, strangled it, and sucked it in. She would have devoured me.

She did.

I leave the Borders in Westwood at five forty-five and drive over the hill into the Valley. There are another fourteen bookstores to visit tonight. And if I don't find her, I will reverse the order and start again in the morning.

But I don't have to.

I find her.

I find her in bookstore number forty-eight, a Bookstar on Ventura and Laurel Canyon, a converted fifties-style movie theatre that still has a large glowing marquee. There's a Starbucks next door.

I'm standing in the New Age section with a Carlos Castaneda book in my hands when I see her. She sits down in an overstuffed chair and starts leafing through a coffee-table book of Monet's

paintings.

I circle around her, through New Age, Philosophy, and Weight Loss. Her hair is pulled back from her face, the way I've always liked, and she is wearing glasses. Her clothes are conservative but expensive: a single-breasted black Donna Karan suit that opens in a V down to her cleavage. There is a Gucci purse tucked between her body and the chair.

She has on all of her jewelry: diamond earrings, gold watch, banded gold necklace.

I can almost smell her.

She flips through her book absently because the hunt is on.

Her chair selection is perfect; its sight lines include the magazine racks and the books on tape.

There are blond streaks in her hair now. I can't get close enough to see her eyes, but I'm sure they are back to blue.

I stand behind her and watch.

She sets down Monet and opens up her purse. She pulls out the front page of today's *Los Angeles Times*.

A burning school bus in full color.

Men walk by her and smile, nod, make their hands look busy. They all do something that makes them obscenely obvious.

They mutter as they pass me.

"Damn," they say.

"Fucking A," they say.

"I love my wife," they say.

But Claire is actually reading. First she reads the front page, the page where I am blamed for the worst case of gridlock in American history. On page three she reads about Armani-man.

Say his name, Lonnie.

She reads about Todd Harris.

Claire.

Say her name, Lonnie.

Hillary Peck removes the commemorative pullout section and reads everything. I watch as she runs her finger through my timeline.

Call 911.

Call your friend Colleen the anchorwoman and tell her that you've got a story for her.

Go find the Yale Shakespeare collection and drop it on Claire, Hillary, whatever the fuck her name is. Drop it right on her head.

She stands up and stretches, takes off her glasses, and rubs her eyes.

A man standing in the Sports Medicine aisle coughs.

A man sitting across from her adjusts his shirt collar.

She picks up her purse and walks toward the door.

I watch her feet.

I watch her legs and her hips and her back and her neck and her head.

Everything is motion. Her hair sways over shoulders, touching briefly, left, right, left, right.

She's the killer.

She's all of the answers.

She's the rule maker.

Claire turns suddenly when she reachs the front door. She waits there for just a moment, drinking in the eyes of all the men who have watched her glide through the bookstore. All the men who, if she wanted them, she could have. She's searing her face into their minds because you can bet she'll be back.

How many times had she stalked me before she finally pounced?

When she finally backs out of the store, it is as though all the gravity on the planet has been sucked out.

White spots start to collide in front of my eyes.

This is an emergency.

Release.

Before you do any real damage to yourself.

Let go, Lonnie.

The time to breathe is now.

There you go.

Now find her. Before you lose her forever.

I run outside in time to see Claire climb into a gold Lexus. She sits in the front seat and pulls her hair down and applies lipstick over a mouth I used to dream about.

Me, I'm sprinting to Charlie's Mustang that I've parked half a block away. I pull in three cars behind her on Ventura and follow her as she weaves down Laurel Canyon toward Hollywood.

I try to remember every episode of *Mannix* I ever saw as I drive. I try to remember how people knew they were being followed. I decide that being indecisive is what does it.

I speed up until I am directly behind her. The bad guys in *Mannix* always hung back a few cars and were always noticed right away.

As we drive through the canyon, I wonder what she's thinking about. Is she thinking about me and what she has done?

Does she envy my fame?

Does she realize that she is as irrelevant as ever and that I am a star? A great big shining star?

Or is she sitting there in her Lexus (paid for by a dead man, I'm certain), wondering which boy will take her to that next level?

I sit in the front seat of Charlie's Mustang and I think about the last month of my life. I think that I don't want to kill Claire, but I want to make her suffer as I have suffered.

There isn't violence in me; I know that now.

Hillary Peck, her name is Hillary Peck. Hillary Peck is going to know suffering. I'm going to tell her the names of every person who has died because of her.

And then I'm going to call the police.

I'm going to tell them I robbed Jim Kochel, I robbed a few restaurants, and I broke into my old apartment. I'm going to hand them all of the information I have on Hillary Peck. I'm going to tell them I don't know anything about all of this other stuff going on in my name.

And then I'm going to find out where my couches are, and my clothes, and I'm going to call my mom and tell her that it's all over and that she can watch TV again without seeing my face.

We get to the bottom of Laurel Canyon and Hillary Peck turns right on Sunset and right again into the parking lot of a bar called the Coconut Teaszer.

I continue past the Teaszer and park my car at Tower Records.

I stare at myself in the rearview mirror.

I've fallen so far in such a short period of time.

I'm so low, I'd need to get the Jaws of Life just to get me to sea level.

It takes me a long time, but I finally recognize myself: My name is Lonnie Milton. I am an account manager for Staff Genius, one of the nation's largest staffing providers. My favorite food is steak cooked medium rare. I wear a size eleven shoe, although I often buy size twelve because my feet tend to swell when I'm under stress. I have a sister named Karen who works at a bank. My mother is kind and generous and worries about me. My best friend is named Charlie. I drive a Toyota Tercel. My favorite baseball team is the Oakland Athletics. I have never been in love with a woman. A woman has never loved me.

If I had it to do all over again, I'd change everything.

Twenty

Claire sits there, flawlessly gorgeous, her hands wrapped around a glass of wine.

How much does it cost to feel beloved?

How much have I sacrificed for this feeling?

The answer sits before me: A fake. A liar. A cheat.

Everything about the Coconut Teaszer is wrong.

A loud band crashes through song after song on a tiny stage.

Men wear leather jackets and drink beer in bottles.

Women wear too much denim.

And then there is Claire: an unbecoming skin on a body that must know it is receding.

Beneath everything else in Claire, in Hillary Peck, is this woman, at this bar. A careless woman who treats men like creatures, like adornments for an outfit, and then slouches back into her own misery or darkness and lets other people worry about the tragedies, the atrocities—and for what?

I could never forgive her or like her or marry her or settle down in a small house in the Valley.

Could I?

Just as I start to back up, to make my way outside to call the police and tell them that everything I have done is justified by an irrelevant woman, Claire turns in her chair and sees me.

"What's the matter, Lonnie? You won't sit and have a drink with me?"

"I know your name," I say. "I know everything."

"There are so many things you need to consider," Claire says.

"You're crazy," I say.

"I'm not the one blowing up the city," Claire says. "I'm not the one who couldn't handle being nobody. Look at you. When I found you, you were nothing. Now you're standing here wearing a thousand-dollar watch and everybody in L.A. knows you."

"Everything you see in the paper, on the news, that's you, Hillary," I say, shouting her first name over the din of the rock band. "You did all of this."

Claire stands up and wags a finger in my face. "I didn't tell you to go into that guy's office and make him off himself. I didn't make you steal a damn thing. Ever heard of free will, Lonnie? Huh? Ever heard of having a fucking spine? You think I haven't had my share of suffering?" She rests her palm on my chest and I want to bite it off at the wrist. "I've been so worried about you, Lonnie. I never meant for any of this to happen."

"Bill Jennings," I say.

"What?"

"That guy at HealthMerge, his name was Bill Jennings," I say. "His wife buried him in a gray suit. His son wore a matching gray suit. His daughter couldn't stop crying through the entire funeral. Bill Jennings's mother threw herself on her son's casket before they could lower it into the ground."

Claire takes her hand from my chest and draws two fingers over her lips. The band on stage announces they are taking a short break and Neil Young starts to play over the PA system.

"Lonnie," she says, "we can sort this all out."

"You set me up for murder," I say. "Just like David Ruttenburg."

Claire's eyes taper into fine slits.

"Didn't Claire Gooden leave you enough money, Hillary?"

Neil Young screams about a thousand points of light in the free world, and Claire tries to storm past me. I grab her by the arm and squeeze the nerve just above her elbow, just like my sister, Karen, used to do to me when we were kids.

"I'm not losing you ever again," I say.

Hillary Peck stands there like a statue; this woman I once thought was a monument. People mill around us, drinking, dancing, and in the middle we are a frozen hurricane.

"Lonnie Milton," Hillary Peck says quietly.

"Lonnie Milton," she says again, her voice rising an octave.

Neil Young is almost done rocking in the free world.

"Lonnie Milton!" she screams as the music fades out.

What happens doesn't happen with words. The Coconut Teaszer swells around us, a hundred different faces press toward mine.

"Lonnie Milton!" she screams again, so I clamp my hand over her mouth. Her tongue licks my palm.

The house lights flicker on and all I see are cell phones. Every guy in a leather jacket has a cell phone in his hand. Every girl in denim dials the same three numbers.

Hillary Peck, who for one perfect night as Claire Gooden made me feel like I was truly beloved, flicks her tongue between my fingers.

People start to fight. Men hit women. Women hit men. Cell phones fly across the room and bounce off of people's heads. A guy with a goatee advances toward me.

The bartender leaps over his bar and smashes the guy in the mouth with a bottle of Rolling Rock.

Blood and teeth spray onto my face.

"Go, Mr. Milton," the bartender says. "I'll hold them off."

Hillary Peck runs her tongue from my pinky all the way to my thumb while I drag her outside to her car.

"Give me the keys," I say.

Sirens.

I hear sirens.

Claire laughs.

"Give me the fucking keys, Claire!"

She says, "Lonnie, this is your time," and drops the keys into my hand. I shove her into the car and she slides across to the passenger side without any hesitation.

We turn left on Sunset into traffic and race toward the freeway. We pass police cars going the opposite direction. They'll turn around soon enough.

"You're going to get caught, Lonnie," she says. "Now you're a kidnapper, too."

Traffic is thick on Sunset, so I have to slow down.

Act like you know what you're doing, I think.

Pretend you are invisible.

You are innocent, Lonnie. Look to your right if you want to see who the police are after.

"I've got you," I say. "It doesn't matter who catches us."

She says, "What do you have? My name in a will? The police don't even know I exist. I don't matter to them, Lonnie. But you left fingerprints all over my boyfriend's house and on that knife. Not to mention all these other stunts you've been pulling."

I look in the rearview mirror and see flashing lights. I hit the gas and swerve into the suicide lane.

I drive like I am Mannix again. I weave in and out of traffic, fishtailing around corners, until I reach the 101 south.

Dozens of police cars follow me onto the freeway, and I know that I am safe for the time being. I'm in a high-speed chase, which means the police won't do a thing to me until I stop the car—especially not with a hostage.

She says, "Let me help you."

The Channel 5 Urgent News chopper zooms over our car and then banks left to get a better angle of my face.

She says, "Let them arrest you. I'll post your bail. I'll get you the finest lawyers money can buy."

"Claire," I say, because that is who she is to me, "you've ruined my life. For nothing."

We hit downtown and I change from the 101 south to the 5 south.

The Action News helicopter darts over Dodger Stadium and swings in beside the Urgent News chopper.

She says, "I didn't want this to happen to you. Never to you. You were different, Lonnie. You know that, right? You must consider that."

"You're a liar, Claire."

Whoop-whoop-whoop.

A police helicopter floods the car with light.

"Lonnie Milton," says a voice from the sky, "pull your automobile over or we will be forced to act."

I've seen this happen on TV before. This means that there are a lot of cars ahead of me and they don't want to see civilians get hurt. My friend Colleen the anchorwoman has said a thousand times that the real danger of these high-speed chases is the reckless driving.

I slow down to sixty-five.

If there were a telephone in this car, I'd call Colleen the anchorwoman at home and let her know that she's done the community a great service with her expert commentary.

Twenty-one

We've been driving south toward Mexico, with fifteen police cars behind us, for almost two hours. There are seven helicopters in the sky. On CNN right now, I'm certain, Bernard Shaw is saying something compelling about me. Saying that I've frozen American commerce with my actions or that I've been responsible for a mass suicide in Kansas or that I used to be considered an employee of some merit at Staff Genius.

She says, "In a different situation, Lonnie, I think we could have been good together."

She says, "You know, at first, I thought it would work with us. I thought that maybe I could settle down with you and have a family even. And then everything fell apart, didn't it?"

She says, "Pejman had a piece in all of this, you know. If he hadn't gotten jealous, none of this would have happened. If he hadn't wanted all of the money for himself."

"Lonnie Milton," says the voice in the sky, "we've given the Mexican government permission to fire at will if you try to cross the border."

She says, "We can make it to Mexico, Lonnie. The American government would never make an agreement like that."

Bernard Shaw is looking down on me from the CNN camera in the sky and he's saying, You know what, Lonnie, I think this Claire girl has you by the short hairs. What *do* you have on her? I'm sick of reporting on this story, Lonnie, and I'm happy to say it looks as if it's about through.

She says, "Have you ever been to Mexico, Lonnie? I spent a summer in a town south of San Felipe called Llano. It's beautiful there, you know. It's not like Tijuana or something. The air smells like cinnamon. And there are women in Llano who sell jicama sprinkled with spices and cook these tender tortillas right on the street. Haven't you always dreamed of a place where you could sit outside all night and watch the stars? My mother used to tell me that stars are like men, Lonnie. Do you believe that?"

I believe that even if I have enough information on Claire, on Hillary Peck, that it won't save me.

Like any of us can be saved.

No matter what happens, I'm going to go to jail.

And now, with sirens flashing in my rearview mirror, with the police ready to shoot me if I make any wrong moves, it doesn't seem so noble to admit my wrongs.

"I've never been to Mexico," I say.

She says, "We could live like royalty in Llano, Lonnie. We really could."

We fly south through Mission Viejo, La Jolla, and San Diego.

People on the side of the road honk their horns, flash their high beams, and wave their hands.

I turn on the radio and all I hear is my name. A DJ on 91X says that he thinks I'll commit suicide before I'm brought in alive and Godspeed to that idea. A talk-show host on KFI says that he hopes I don't do something crazy like kill my hostage.

My hostage has her hand on my thigh.

KCBS cuts into a taped interview with Julie to deliver a live interview with my mother.

Claire says, "Turn it off, Lonnie."

But I turn it up.

My mom says, "If you're listening, Lonnie, please just let that poor woman go. She hasn't done anything to you. We love you and we miss you and we know that you're just sick, Lonnie. Please pull your car over, please honey, before more people get hurt."

No one else is getting hurt.

My mom tells me again how much she loves me, but I change the station anyway. I can't go back. I don't want to go back.

On KFI, the host says that the police are putting spikes in the road to stop my car. He says that Mexican officials have refused to comply with a request to close down the border crossing in Tijuana. Because, the host says, of an incident only a few days ago where a man in a blue Impala was arrested and beaten at the border after a similar chase and is now suing the Mexican government for 7 billion dollars.

She says, "There are so many things we need to consider, Lonnie."

The only thing left to consider is this: Do I go through the rest of my life knowing I failed to achieve some promise, some ascendancy to greatness, that moment everyone dreams of? Do I ponder my life between three walls and metal bars and think that the only mistake I ever made was giving up?

Or do I drive over the spikes in the road with a killer by my side, with a woman who sold my fate because I am as irrelevant as she was.

I look at the killer and I say her name over and over again in my head. Her hand caresses the inside of my thigh and I say her name.

A sign says that we are four miles from the border.

I memorize her skin.

A caller on KFI says that no matter what happens to me, if the police kill me or if the Mexicans kill me or if I slip away like D. B. Cooper, everything I've set in motion will go on. The caller, his name is Jim and he's calling from Palm Springs, says that in the future my word will be spread through computer viruses, a complex network of organized restaurant mayhem, and origami.

My word will live as a paper swan.

Ahead of us, police cars are blockaded across the freeway. My headlights pick up the glint of metal spikes on the road.

Jim from Palm Springs says that my army is mobilizing near the border at this very moment. He says that for every five police officers who want me dead, there are another ten officers who would swallow glass for me.

I flash my brights to let my people know that I am coming.

Open the road.

I am here to save you.

Claire puts on a fresh coat of lipstick.

I press down on the gas and the speedometer jumps to 80.

90.

100.

The police cars will spread apart just wide enough to let us slip through. Claire and I will melt into the sea of humanity at the border while my people close ranks behind us.

We are three hundred yards from the blockade.

Have I gotten what I wanted from this world?

She says, "Yes, Lonnie."

Do we really have a future?

She says, "Yes, Lonnie."

150.

Do you love me, Claire? Do you really love me?

She says, "Yes, Lonnie."

75.

Tell me about Mexico again, Claire. Tell me how we'll be like royalty.

She says, "I will, Lonnie. Just drive."

And I do.

MUSIC TELEVISION

POCKET
BOOKS